David John Banner was born in 1939 in rural Worcestershire, the third son of the village butcher in Aston Fields, Bromsgrove.

Following an education at Bromsgrove County High School he has worked for his entire life in the food and farming industries.

Married to Jill for fifty-one years, they have three sons and four grandchildren. In 1995 David was appointed a magistrate to the Bromsgrove and Redditch Bench serving as a Bench Chairman until 2007.

All Is Safely Gathered In

David Banner

All Is Safely Gathered In

Vanguard Press

VANGUARD PAPERBACK

© Copyright 2011
David Banner

The right of David Banner to be identified as author of
this work has been asserted by him in accordance with the
Copyright, Designs and Patents Act 1988.

All Rights Reserved

No reproduction, copy or transmission of this publication
may be made without written permission.
No paragraph of this publication may be reproduced,
copied or transmitted save with the written permission of the publisher, or
in accordance with the provisions
of the Copyright Act 1956 (as amended).

Any person who commits any unauthorised act in relation to
this publication may be liable to criminal
prosecution and civil claims for damages.

All the characters in this book are imaginary. Any resemblance to anyone
living or dead or to situations that may have occurred are coincidental.

A CIP catalogue record for this title is
available from the British Library.

ISBN 978 1 84386 930 6

Vanguard Press is an imprint of
Pegasus Elliot MacKenzie Publishers Ltd.
www.pegasuspublishers.com

First Published in 2011

Vanguard Press
Sheraton House Castle Park
Cambridge England

Printed & Bound in Great Britain

Acknowledgements

To Josephine Hearn, Kevin Cassidy, Jim Page MBE, Frances Page, Trevor Higgingbottom JP and Margaret Lunnon who all read early drafts and gave much useful advice and encouragement.

Also to Paul Vaughan JP for his advice.

A special thanks to Judy Bate, my sister-in-law an indefatigable typist.

To 'The Talking Books for the Blind Service'
to whom a contribution from the net sale of each book will
be made, by the author.

*And to the memory of Emily and Eric, my mother and
father.*

An English Country Landscape

Greens satin soft and softer yet
Lie easy on the eye.

Quiet still and still, a timeless hush
'cept winds that barely sigh.

Patchwork scenes of green and greens
smudged with shimmering gold,

Glorious pastoral splendour
earth's paradise unfold.

So calm and grand yon verdant scene,
creation nigh sublime,

Whilst pause and feast your avid eye
there's no such thing as time.

So linger, gape and wonder – serenity behold;
your eye should frame this masterpiece
and sear it on your soul.

D.J.B.

CHAPTER ONE

AMPLEFORD, ENGLAND, 1958

It was cold. God, it was cold. The market traders were busily packing their wares in readiness for a sharp getaway at 5 o'clock. Already it was dark, and the lights and lamps were twinkling along the streets and lanes that stretched through Ampleford from the old market hall.

There had been a market on the site for over five hundred years. The hall, built in early Victorian England, made little gesture to comfort or warmth. What was a blessing in the steamy months of July and August, when the cool draughts brought temperatures down to levels that helped to preserve the produce, was a curse on this bitter February afternoon as the cruel northeast wind swept through the hall, chilling everyone and everything to biting levels. A frost rime was forming on the vans and cars outside. As people spoke, their breath hung in clouds, and mountainous banks of grey-black snowflakes swirled across the town on the gathering wind.

Seventeen-year-old Mary glanced for the umpteenth time at the market clock. It was 4.35 p.m. – another twenty-five minutes before George would collect her. She had sold three hundred dozen eggs for one shilling and two pence a dozen, plus a few of her 'bits and bobs' as she called them – eight boiling fowl and fourteen home-made cakes.

Customers were sparse by now, virtually non-existent, as she blew on her fingers and stamped her feet to keep the circulation flowing through her slight, young limbs. She silently had a little moan at the council's byelaws that obliged the traders to remain in position until 5 o'clock. Unlike the purveyors of pots and pans, baskets, clothes, shoes, and so on, she always sold out. She had nothing left to sell or pack away to take home, but she must always remain in place until 5 o'clock when the market superintendent would collect the council's toll of £2 for Saturday trading.

Mary had the grand sum of £24 in her little cash box, including the £1/10s float she had started with. The box was on the table behind the main trestle on which she displayed her eggs. Suddenly, as if from nowhere, he appeared – a mean, spotty-faced, runt of a man. She had not seen him until he swept round the corner of the tea and sandwich wagon which stood alongside Mary's simple stall. Quick as a viper's tongue, he scooped her cash box into the hook of his forearm and under his coat. He fled through the hall, jumping and side-stepping the market jumble as he went – her cries of "Stop him, stop him, thief, stop him", ringing across the stalls and walkways.

At the bottom end of the market hall by the rear entrance, skirted by the town brook, Molly Perkins ran a fruit and vegetable stall. Most of her produce was home grown on her own market garden. She was helped by her son, Billy, now nineteen years old, who was a six-footer, sixteen stone, and as thick as the proverbial shovel. Billy had no mental illness – he was just slow and simple. Reading and writing he had never mastered, but give him a pile of stakes, a roll of wire, a sledge hammer and a spade, and he would put up as good a fence as any man. His work on the land, growing his mother's potatoes, lettuce, cauliflowers, and more, had honed his body to formidable levels of strength and fitness.

The sneaky thief sped through the market hall and was just leaving the rear entrance to cross the footbridge over the town brook as Billy, loading sacks of potatoes on to his mother's van, parked in the rear car park, heard the piercing screech of his mother's voice. "Stop him, Billy, he's got Mary's money. Stop the swine, down him." Billy stuck his leg out as he went past, sending him sprawling across the planks of the little bridge. He only half-rose as Billy picked him off the ground, like a bulldog with a mouse. His clenched fist swung and smashed his jaw to a grotesque angle and as he fell, for good measure, Billy's right foot, hob-nailed boot and all, thudded sickeningly into his right ear. He lay motionless, except for the slight twitching of his left leg, with blood trickling from his ear, nose and mouth. Billy retrieved Mary's cash box from the brook and, with a satisfied grin on his face, like the cat that had stolen the cream, he handed it gently to his mother. "Christ, Billy," she said, "what the hell have you done? We only said stop him."

"Get an amberlance," Bob Merrick cried, "he's f, f, f, f, fuckin' dead he is, fuckin' dead as m, m, m, m, mutton, he is," stammered Bob. At that moment, he stammered the truth. Runty little sneak thief had crossed the great divide from which there is no return – Billy had stopped him alright, he had stopped him for good.

Rapidly a huddle of people gathered round the stricken thief. "Purra blanket or summut under his yed," someone yelled.

"Wot for? Make no bleedin' difference to him," came a reply.

"I know him," piped up Jack Lees, "he's one of the Radleys from Chesterton, his brother's in jail fer burglin', an' his ole man's bin inside, right bad lot they am. He's bin creepin' round the market for a wik or two, slimey little bastard, he's in the right place now, fer sure."

An ambulance, followed swiftly by a police car, came clanging up to the scene as someone with some presence of mind had weighed up the seriousness of the mishap and dialled 999. Gary Radley's body was duly loaded and some fifteen, fleeting, ferocious minutes after his attempted snatch, he was on the way to Ampleford Cottage Hospital, where a doctor pronounced him dead on arrival, and he was laid to rest in the mortuary.

Mary Jones was worried. George Evans collected her promptly at 5 o'clock in the farm truck. George, now in his seventies, was mithering about the state of the roads although it was only two miles back to Crest Farm, and the snow had not yet settled to any degree. George was Harry Evans' bachelor brother; both had been born on the farm that had been in their family's ownership for nearly a century. Whilst Harry had married and fathered a daughter, George had led a contented, genteel life, looking after the livestock and reading quietly in his own room which somehow, over the years, had developed into his sanctuary. His reading often included the Bible – he was a stalwart attender at St Mark's. In recent years, errands, like taking Mary to market on Saturday mornings and picking her up in the afternoons, were typical of his dwindling involvement at the farm. In the ten short minutes their journey took, Mary regaled the tragic details of her afternoon. She was racked with anxiety and apprehension, Billy's feeble words during their parting conversation still ringing in her ears. "I stopped him, Mair, I stopped him. I got yer money back for yer didn't I, Mair."

"Thanks, Billy, thanks, now go with the policeman. I'll come and see you directly, as soon as I've seen all the chicks are shut up tight. I'll only be an hour or so, now jus' behave, trust me, and I'll see you very soon." She had squeezed his hand, he was pacified, Mary was coming soon, she'd never let him down, and his mom was following behind in the van.

George Evans dropped Mary off at the end of the drive to Crest Farm. She had a short, fifty yards walk down the path, through the orchard to the sandstone cottage where she lived with her grandfather, Jack Berry, her father, Dick, and his sister, Aunty Jo. Jack had lived in the farm cottage on a tied tenancy for fifty years with his beloved Rose and they had been blessed with a lovely daughter, Joan, Mary's mother.

AMPLEFORD 1946

Twelve years earlier, nothing in their previous lives could have prepared them for the tragic events that were about to unfold. Jack had celebrated his sixty-eighth birthday in the January of that year, but the post war moods of relief and deliverance following the Allies' victory were soon shattered in the Berry's home. Everyone knew that Rose had heart problems – irregular rhythm and a faulty valve. The doctor had told her so some ten years before. "Just don't overdo things and take two of the pills, one in the morning, one in the evening," was all he could offer. Rose had a check-up every six months, and the last one in November had revealed nothing new.

It was Sunday morning, the first week in March. Jack had risen at 5.30 a.m., as he'd done for the last fifty years, washed and shaved in the little washhouse at the rear of the cottage, lit the fire in the parlour, and re-climbed the narrow stairs with cups of tea for baby Mary and her mom and dad, and one for Rose with her tablet in the saucer. As soon as he had set the tea down on the little cupboard beside her bed and turned to Rose, he knew. Her eyes were open but seeing nothing, her lips were blue, set in a face with an ashen grey complexion, and her right arm dangled uselessly over the side of the bed. The position of her leg indicated that she had been about to get out of bed but her weakened heart, objecting to the demands of her body, had stopped, and in the split second it takes to put a light out, Rose, gentle, kind Rose, had gone to the heaven to which she undoubtedly belonged. Rose was also sixty-eight and their marriage had spanned forty-five years, years of blissful, domestic harmony.

During the early weeks of grief and mourning, Jack recalled their shared joy at the birth of their daughter, Joan, and repeated, on numerous occasions, tales of her early upbringing and their satisfaction and welcoming of Dick Jones into their family in 1936, as their son-in-law. To begin with, Dick had worked part time at Crest Farm but was now Farm Manager in everything but title, and had assumed the tied cottage tenancy into his name. The birth of little Mary in 1941 had set the seal on this happy, hardworking, honest, little family, and in spite of the comment that "it'd be nice to see a lad one of these days", Jack loved the little lass dearly.

Almost as soon as Rose Berry had died, within three weeks or so, Joan had started to lose weight. Gradually her clothes became loose and her cheekbones and chin became more prominent. Her appetite was fine, although she noticed that the household chores and her tasks with the poultry round the farm were leaving her increasingly breathless. Early comments were made by Joan's sister-in-law, Mary's Aunty Jo, who came visiting on her bike every Saturday afternoon. Dick's elder spinster sister, whose real name was Barbara Jones, was the district nurse and midwife. Mary, aged two, had called her Aunty Jones, shortened to Aunty Jo in her baby gabble, and Aunty Jo it was forever more.

"Joan, you've lost a bit of weight since your mom died. Do you feel any better for it?" Aunty Jo commented.

"Trust you to notice. No, I don't as a matter of fact, I feel terrible, so damned tired all the time somehow. It'll pass, just the stress of Mom's job I reckon, and looking after Dad and all."

"Get yourself down to the surgery and see Dr Powell. He'll give you something to help, perhaps," advised Aunty Jo.

"Oh, I'll see, don't want to go fussin' at the doctor's 'cos I'm tired. He'll think I'm some sort of nutcase."

"Now, listen to me, Joan, when I come next Saturday I'll tell you what day and what time you are going. When I see the doctor on Monday I'll make an appointment for you for the following week. Now don't argue!"

Joan didn't argue; she felt an inner relief as Aunty Jo said her goodbyes and left. Aunty Jo's instinctive nurse's eye had spotted the slightest hint of yellow in Joan's eyes. Jaundice bellowed through her brain – the weight loss and the fatigue. She pedalled her bicycle home with a heavy heart, hoping against hope that what she was thinking was wrong, that she was mistaken. Little Mary was barely five years old, Joan was only thirty-four, for God's sake – and Grandad and Dick – God wouldn't do such a thing. Aunty Jo swallowed hard at the lump in her throat and fought hard to keep back the tears as she put her bike into the shed and let herself into her little terraced cottage in Lower Street. "God wouldn't do such a thing to such innocent, peaceful people, would he?" She knew the answer – she was a midwife – he certainly would! She had often struggled in her mind with the workings of the Almighty. She had delivered hundreds of babies during her career in

Ampleford, and inevitably had her share of stillborn misfortunes – perfectly formed little bundles with not a breath in their body, destined by custom to an unmarked burial up against the boundary wall of St Mark's churchyard. How did God choose, and why was she now, in spite of the faith that took her to Communion every Sunday morning, doubting that he would take care of her dear brother, Dick, her baby niece, Mary, kind gentle Joan, and her ageing father?

Spiritually, Joan and Aunty Jo were as close as real sisters, but there any similarity ended. Joan was a dainty five feet three inches tall with sparkling blue eyes, light brown hair that crowned a pretty face, and a soft, curvy figure. Aunty Jo was her brother Dick's image in a nurse's outfit, five feet ten, lantern-jawed, short cropped black hair, and lower legs developed by the bike-riding around the town into replica milk bottles. Joan oozed delicious femininity – Aunty Jo did not, and yet she was revered by the people of Ampleford.

As well as her duties as a midwife, her work with the sick and dying attracted great respect and love from everyone. Some years before she had been called upon to clean up after the suicide of a local farmer who had put a shot gun into his mouth and blown his brains out all over the kitchen ceiling. Aunty Jo set to with gusto and left the place spotless before trudging off on her bike to deliver a baby.

The local youngsters sometimes looked upon her as a figure of fun as she cycled round the town, revealing her long knickers stretching down to her knees. "Droopy drawers, nurse droopy drawers," they would cry as she shook her fist at them, shouting back, "Cheeky monkeys, brought most of you into this world, I did." One of the main participants in this cat-calling was a fifteen-year-old lad called Barry Lane. Barry contracted tonsillitis and Aunty Jo was required to call at his home daily to give him a course of penicillin injections. Aunty Jo never revealed what went on, she was far too professional, but she did say afterwards, "Them lads ain't so bold with their insults since I gave Barry Lane his treatment with the needle."

Aunty Jo and Joan were soul mates. They often recalled the war time nights when Dick would work the late, vital shifts at the farm. Joan, pregnant with Mary, would enjoy Aunty Jo's company late into the evening, waiting for Dick's exhausted return. A bottle of homemade rhubarb wine was comfort divine. The alcohol would change Aunty Jo into a "right old giggle", Joan recalled. When Joan asked the question, "What will the birth of my baby really be like?" Aunty Jo had replied, "Haven't the faintest idea. Never had one nor ever will. I've put stitches into half the fannies in Ampleford, and you'd be surprised how many of them are only blondes till you get their drawers down, but if you want to know what it's really like, ask somebody who's had one. Better still, wait and see!" Coming from prim and proper Aunty Jo, who never used a swear word in the normal course of things, this mild coarseness had reduced them both to fits of tearful laughter. Joan had taken her advice – she'd wait and see.

Joan's appointment with Dr Powell came on the Monday of the following week. "Take a sample of wee with you," Aunty Jo had told her. Dr Powell examined her and also took a sample of blood from her arm.

"Something is making you a bit jaundiced, Mrs Jones," he said. "We need to do tests on this urine sample and your blood. I shall have the results on Thursday, so come and see me again on Thursday evening and we'll see if we can sort you out. In the meantime, try to take it easy."

On the Thursday evening, Joan entered the doctor's consulting room with great trepidation. She wasn't getting any better, that was for sure. "Now, Mrs Jones," he began, "the results of the tests are not conclusive but I must be honest with you – they are not encouraging. I want you to go into Chesterton General Hospital next Tuesday for a few days. You will be under the care of Dr Long there. He is a liver specialist and will do several more tests with X-rays and so on, and, hopefully, get you sorted out."

"Have you any idea what might be the matter with me, Doctor?" Joan asked. "Please tell me what your thoughts are, and what the possibilities may be."

"Well, I think it is possible that you may have something obstructing the pancreatic duct, Mrs Jones, but I can't be one hundred per cent sure."

Joan looked him straight in the eye. "Are you telling me that I might have cancer, Dr Powell?" she asked. "I'm not daft, Doctor, I can see what's happening with my weight and all."

"I cannot be sure, Mrs Jones, without further extensive tests. I cannot confirm anything, nor rule anything out and I'm sorry if I sound vague. I'm not avoiding the issue but let's get these other tests out of the way and then a solid diagnosis will be possible. Next Tuesday then. You should have a letter on Monday morning, but if not ring the surgery." He gave Joan a prescription, "something to help you sleep and calm you down a bit".

Joan did sleep quite well with the help of the tablets. She busied herself around the cottage and amongst the poultry in the orchard, as much as her increasing fatigue would allow.

On Sunday evening she strolled gently, hand in hand with little Mary, the half mile or so to the little spinney at the very highest point of Crest Farm and sat herself down on the trunk of the fallen tree, the spot where she and Dick had first held hands and first kissed – a spot that had become very special to them. Mary was happily picking the cowslips to take home to Gramps. Joan scooped her softly on to her lap and gazed across the endless, rolling April landscape upon which a watery, spring sun was setting. She had known this spot for her entire life, and had never perceived it quite so beautiful, had never seen the gentle, rolling contours resting so comfortably. The soft mid-April greens sat perfectly against the blushing evening sky, with the sharp detail of the little farms and the distant Ampleford rooftops merging in a creation of breathtaking beauty. She watched the baby lambs racing and gambolling up and down the slopes in a frenzy of joyous playtime, whilst their dignified mams placidly contented themselves to the task of converting the fresh spring grasses into the rich milk that was the fuel for their rapturous display. She drew Mary closely to her body in a gentle hug, and ran her fingers through the profusion of soft auburn curls that tumbled around her tiny face. She traced a path with her forefinger from freckle to freckle across the bridge of the pudgy little nose, half closing her eyes and whispering, "Please, please, God, take care of this tiny lamb, please – just – take – great – great – care."

Joan had said very little to Dick about her visits to Dr Powell, and he was stunned by her news that she was booked into Chesterton General on Tuesday. "God, Joany, is there something serious?" he asked.

"He doesn't know," Joan replied, "needs more tests and X-rays he says. Dick, we've just got to get on with it."

Saturday came and Auntie Jo arrived, as usual, on her bike, dressed as always in her navy blue midwife's dress with stiff, starched white collar and cuffs, and her navy blue gabardine mackintosh. She knew of Joan's imminent admission to Chesterton General from her close daily contact with Dr Powell. Never one for skirting around things, Aunty Jo came straight to the point. "Now listen, Joan, when you go to Chesterton on Tuesday, I'm going to move in here for a day or two." Joan motioned to protest. "No argument," continued Aunty Jo, "there's nothing else for it. I've got a week's leave due and you can settle yourself down in the knowledge that everyone here is being properly tended to. I'll be up on Tuesday morning, then we'll all come to see you on Tuesday night."

Joan hugged her sister-in-law for all she was worth, with as much strength as her weakening limbs could muster. "Bless you, our Barbara," she whispered. "God bless you, Aunty Jo."

There was an empty, hollow sort of atmosphere around the cottage over that weekend as Joan and Dick both struggled to keep her impending hospital stay in the back corners of their minds. The normality for which they both strived was helped by Dick being on weekend milking duty and his conscientious tending of the ewes and lambs. Joan laboured to get all the washing up to date, change all the beds, and on the Monday bake a big fruit cake and enough little cakes to fill a big, old biscuit tin. No amount of sleep seemed to make any difference now – Joan was reaching into her deepest reserves to keep going and it showed. Apart from the weight loss and jaundice, her eyes were now deep, dark hollows.

On the Monday morning Joan had watched the little red post van turn the corner at the bottom of the hill, about three quarters of a mile away. She saw it stop at Molly Perkins' place half way up the hill, and then lost sight of it until it went past the bottom of the path and up the drive to Crest Farm with mail for the Evans'. On the way back it stopped.

Don, the postman, came scampering up the path with her letter:

'Dear Mrs Jones,

After a referral by Dr Powell of Ampleford Surgery, a bed has been reserved for you in Ward 18 from Tuesday April 16th. You will be under the care of Dr Long. Please present yourself between 11.30 a.m. and 12 noon.'

There was a list of the usual things for her to take and things she could not take, like alcohol, cigarettes, and so on; also an expression of hope that she would find her stay in Chesterton General Hospital as comfortable as circumstances would allow.

Joan's dad hadn't really cottoned on to the situation yet. He was still in a state of mourning and heartache for his beloved Rose about whom he kept saying, "Was taken too soon, didn't have her proper span. I can't understand why a woman like yer mother had to die so young."

Joan had seen him watching her read the letter. "Oh dear, Dad," she said, "this is a damned nuisance. I've got to go into hospital for a few days for some tests, into Chesterton General on Tuesday. Aunty Jo's coming up to look after things for a while, what with Mary and all, so you'll be alright 'till I come back." Thus Joan quietly softened her dad's learning of the situation.

Jack Berry had kept dogs throughout his career at Crest Farm. He had arrived there as a twenty-year-old with a little collie bitch, bought for one shilling and six pence at Ampleford Fair, bought whilst he was 'merry', even drunk. He named her Connie and she became Con for short. He trained her with the sheep and she became his close, working partner in the fields, an invaluable, almost irreplaceable, mate. Con lived until she was twelve, and by an arranged mating with Zip, a border collie working on a neighbouring farm, she left Jack with a lovely bitch puppy,

Lottie. So Jack Berry's collies came tumbling down the generations to his present dog, Hettie, which he reckoned 'was the best of the lot' – mind you, he always said that! Each one of his bitches was allowed one family at four or five years old, but only two puppies were ever reared, one to keep the line going and one to sell. Jack's chosen pups, always bitches, would then be out in the fields at four or five months old, shadowing their mother who would be obeying Jack's calls and whistles. Thus they were easily trained to Jack's ways and the ways of the sheep, and became invaluable members of the farm staff. Jack loved his collies – he was proud of their capabilities, and neighbouring farmers would often voice to Harry Evans their envy of Jack's abilities. "That Jack Berry's a diamond you know, Harry. Don't know what you pay him but his dogs alone are worth a man's wage."

"I look after him," Harry would reply. Harry knew that Jack would never leave Crest Farm for any amount of wages. He had lived and worked there for fifty years and he not only loved the place but was deeply entrenched in its soil, in the gentle rhythm of the seasons. Crest Farm was his world, his reason for existing. Harry Evans often thought of his father's words, "You'll never have a better man than Jack Berry, not if you live to be two hundred, let alone one." Old Mr Evans had given Jack the job, put him in the cottage, and showed respect, admiration, and gratitude for his quiet, gentle skills with horses, cattle and sheep.

Hettie had recently had a litter of nine pups, just a week before Rose's death. Dick had sensibly dispatched seven of them back to their maker, via a sack bag, sunk with a brick into the farm pond. The thought of nine puppies growing up and running round the cottage was an impractical nightmare. Jack had selected two tiny little bitches to rear, still not much more than blind foetuses, both heavily marked with white – Splash and Patch they became. By now they were eight weeks old, full of mischief and fun, and a great delight to Jack and little Mary who squealed with pleasure as she scampered round the orchard with them, pulling their tails and tickling their tummies. The puppies' timely arrival was a great therapy for Jack. At least his mind was not dwelling on his recent bereavement, and the puppies gave him some element of continuity to cling to. He not only looked back over the decades to Con, their ancestor, and her subsequent progeny, but he also looked forward to next summer when Splash and Patch would be running in the fields with Hettie, learning their trade. Whilst painfully absorbing the finality of Rose's death, the puppies showed him a future and he clung to it.

Tuesday morning came. Joan had filled the zinc bath in the scullery with hot water from the electric boiler, locked the back door and drawn the curtains. Dick had gone to work about an hour ago, and her Dad was feeding the hens in the orchard, a gentle task that would occupy him for an hour or so. They would both be in for breakfast about 8.30 a.m., giving her a good hour to herself as Mary was still asleep. Joan lowered herself gently into the soapy water and looked down in dismay at her shrivelled breasts and limbs. Her healthy, cuddly, ten stone frame was now weighing somewhere below a withering eight stones. She lay back to soak up the caressing warmth of the water, and reluctantly admitted to herself that she was pleased she was going into hospital. Joan had always had an abundance of common sense and she knew that things could not go on; she knew that she needed help, urgently and desperately.

Aunty Jo came up on her bike at 9.30 a.m. and was given her instructions by Joan. "They always have two slices of bacon, two eggs, and two rounds of toast for their breakfast Mary has a boiled egg. Don't worry about dinner time – they'll help themselves to a bit of cold meat or cheese, with bread and pickles. At night it's usually something out of the pot on the stove with boiled potatoes. We always have a brisket of beef for roast on Sunday, cold on Monday with bubble and squeak, and then I put the bone in the pot on the stove with plenty of carrots and onions for Tuesday night. The butcher's van will call tomorrow with some belly pork and sausages, and Dad will find a rabbit or two, or a boiling fowl, for the pot on Friday. Saturday night we always have eggs on toast and tinned beans, what with them having a big Sunday lunch to look forward to."

"What about the dogs?" asked Aunty Jo.

"A dish of milk in the mornings – Dick will see to that – drop a couple of the soft shelled eggs into it, and make sure you've got an extra few potatoes to mash up for them at night with some gravy out of the pot on the stove. They'll eat all the scraps and the butcher boy will bring a good bag of bones tomorrow and again on Saturday."

With everything settled in her mind, Joan kissed Mary and her dad, hugged Aunty Jo and, with her bag of belongings, climbed into the farm van which Dick had borrowed for a couple of hours.

The thirty minute ride to Chesterton was uneventful, and apart from Joan saying, "I shall never be out of your Barbara's debt", little passed between them. Joan was put into a side ward off Ward 18, a room of her own. She was frustrated to be told by Sister that she must first have a bath before she could get into bed. Her protests that she'd had a bath barely four hours ago were sympathetically dismissed.

"I do believe you," said the sister, "you look as fresh as a new pin but it is a hospital rule. All new admissions go straight into the bath. Matron would skin me if I let you get away with it."

Joan took another bath and settled back into her bed. The little room was pristine, everything shone and sparkled, and the bed sheets were crisp and snow white. Joan approved – she was at home with cleanliness and she was comfortable. The closed door afforded peace and quiet and soon her grateful body seized upon the opportunity for sleep. She slept the sleep of the Gods and dreamt the dreams of angels. She dreamt of summer days and sunshine, of April showers that festooned the skies with a hundred rainbows. She dreamt of Crest Farm cottage, her home, of the garden, a kaleidoscope of colour with the old cabbage roses rambling up the walls entwined with honeysuckle and ivy, the borders a riot of hollyhocks, lupins, foxgloves and cornflowers. She saw the orchard awash with buttercups and cowslips as, hand-in-hand with Mary, she floated gently through the fields – fields with no cowpats or puddles, no thistles or nettles, banks with no brambles. In her dreams, she and Mary were both toddlers, the same age. They helped her dad with his plum wine. They helped her mother bottling the autumn pears and damsons. They ate home-baked bread, spread with butter and honey, and they laughed until the fields echoed with the joyous sound of their innocent mirth. She dreamt of her mother standing at the back door with her flowery pinafore on, "Come on you two, your dad'll be home directly, playtime's over, time for supper, time for bed."

Thirty years before, when Joan was a toddler, her mother had shown her how to make daisy chains in the orchard, and how to blow dandelion clocks. She had done exactly the same things with Mary, releasing a million little parachutes to drift across the Crest Farm meadows on the summer breezes. In her dreams she, too, was floating and drifting free, like the dandelion seeds, but now her own tiny parachute was falling gently down to the grass.

As she slowly emerged from her slumbers and surfaced into the real world of Ward 18, she was conscious of someone stroking the back of her hand. Dr Long, a tall, balding man in his late forties, peered down at her through his heavily rimmed spectacles. It was 5 o'clock.

"Hello, Mrs Jones, did I disturb you? My word, you were well away there, I was just about to leave and come back later." Joan was instantly at ease. "We shall be taking you down the corridor tomorrow for an X-ray. I should get the plates on Thursday morning and I will come and see you again on Thursday evening."

"What do you think might be the matter with me?" asked Joan.

"Well, there are several possibilities – I haven't ruled out gallstones except they usually bring on bouts of severe sharp pain, and I understand you haven't suffered in that way."

"Actually," Joan replied, "in the last couple of days I have started to hurt inside a bit, like a smarting, burning sort of feeling."

"Let's wait until after tomorrow," Dr Long said slowly, with a gentle, sympathetic smile on his face. "Let's hope for the best. We shall be doing everything we can to get you better, but in the meantime we'll give you something to ease that burning feeling you mentioned."

At 7 o'clock that night, Dick, Aunty Jo and Mary came visiting. Mary was mostly concerned with drinking her mother's water, eating her biscuits and playing with the bedside wireless earphones. Joan hugged her bye-bye, told her to be a good girl for Aunty Jo, and that it was way past her bedtime. On the Wednesday evening, Mary stayed with her grandad. The previous late night had taken its toll and she needed little persuasion by Aunty Jo to go to 'beddy-byes', after crayoning a card with flowers and matchstick men and ladies for mommy.

Dick and Aunty Jo entered Joan's room and both were stunned by the deterioration from the day before. She could barely lift her head, her face was yellow-straw coloured, she was obviously deeply uncomfortable and beads of perspiration stood out on her brow. She managed to tell them she had been X-rayed and that she had hurt like hell inside until they had given her something.

"God, Barb," said Dick as he drove the farm van back home. "She looked bloody rough to me tonight. I reckon she's going to need an operation or something before she gets right."

"She's in the right place, Dick, that's for sure," replied his sister, "that Dr Long's got a marvellous reputation. Whatever he says or does will be right, you can rest assured." She didn't see the point in telling him the dreadful possibilities.

"It don't seem fair somehow, Barb, that we've got to handle all this so soon after her mom. Thank the Lord we've got you to turn to," Dick added.

"Look, Dick, I'll do all I can for as long as I'm needed. You'd do the same for me now, wouldn't you?"

His left hand left the steering wheel and squeezed his sister's thigh. "Goes without saying really, don't it Barb."

On the following day when Dick returned to the farmyard from his midday break to continue with the chores, Mrs Evans called him over to the house. "There's a 'phone message for you, Dick. Can you meet Dr Long in his room at the hospital at 6.45 this evening? I do hope everything is alright."

Nancy Evans, Harry's wife, was roughly the same age as Joan, being thirteen years younger than Harry. They had a daughter, Elizabeth, seven years old and in her second year at school. Nancy was a leading light in the Ampleford WI, and in St Mark's Young Mothers' Union, being chairwoman of the latter. Joan had always noticed that in her rare meetings with Nancy, or Mrs Evans as she always called her, she always avoided any mention of these ladies' groups which obviously meant so much to her, and took up so much of her time. Other women had, on several occasions, suggested to Joan that she might like to join the WI, and the vicar himself, at Mary's christening, had said, "I do hope we will see you at our Young Mothers' group now, Mrs Jones."

Nancy Evans had simply never said a word to her closest neighbour on these matters, and Joan took the view that "if Mrs Evans doesn't ask me, Mrs Evans doesn't want me". It didn't hurt Joan's feelings or worry her unduly – she was too nice-natured for that, and life was full and busy anyway. She did sometimes think in her quietest moments that being the daughter of a farm labourer, and now married to a farm labourer, perhaps her face didn't fit, and that Mrs Evans wanted her own space on the other side of the social playing field. Joan had mentioned it to Aunty Jo once, saying, "I couldn't care less really, but it's so obvious she doesn't want me involved. On the odd occasion I have mentioned St Marks or the WI, she either changes the subject or shuts up like a clam."

"Don't let it worry you, love," said Aunty Jo, "you'd cramp her style when she starts up with all her airs and graces, with her swanky lah de dah chums, that's what it is. I've seen most of them with their knickers off. I've been inside their houses and their bedrooms, dirty sods some of 'em, I can tell you. You're better than all that lot put together, Joan. Believe me, you're well off without them."

Dick was accompanied by his sister once more, as they climbed the stairs to the third floor at Chesterton General and made their way along the corridors to Dr Long's consulting room. There was a simple reception area with bench seats on two sides, and a table with some flowers and glossy magazines on it. Two other people were waiting, but almost as soon as they entered, a tall, smartly dressed lady emerged from a side office and inquired, "Mr Jones, is it?"

That's right," he replied.

"Dr Long is expecting you, please come through." They walked into a large room with an examination couch up against one wall. Dr Long was seated at a huge oak desk, immaculate in his dark suit, white shirt and red tie, with a face that shone with good health and wholesomeness. "This is your sister, Nurse Jones, I presume?"

"That's right, Doctor, my sister Barbara."

The doctor continued, "Dr Powell tells me that you are his mainstay down in Ampleford, Nurse Jones. He says you are his right hand and speaks very highly of your work."

"That's nice of him," Aunty Jo replied shortly, never one for flattery. Dr Long's face then took on a different countenance, one of gravity and sadness and he began to speak. "Mr Jones, I have to give you the dreadful news that your wife is dying with cancer of the pancreas." One simple, devastating sentence shattered Dick into a thousand pieces.

"Dying, Doctor?" he whispered, "dying, are you quite sure?" His lips trembled as the colour drained from his face. "Are you certain?"

Dr Long brought his hands up and placed them on the desk in front of him. "I'm sorry to be so abrupt but there are no easy words in these circumstances, and I have always found it best to come straight to the honest truth. I am as certain as anyone could be. I really am most dreadfully sorry, her condition is untreatable."

"Is there nothing anyone can do, Doctor?" Dick asked, the words gasping from his lips. By now Aunty Jo, sitting to his right, had reached across and clasped his right hand into hers, with her left arm draped lightly on his shoulder.

"Absolutely nothing I'm afraid. The tumour is quite large and quite advanced. Fluids that should be leaving her liver are trapped there. To remove the tumour would in itself bring about death – her liver is simply unable to drain. The condition is terminal I am sorry to say."

"How long has she got, Doctor?" asked Dick.

"Not much more than a week in my experience," replied Dr Long.

"A week," gasped Dick.

"I have no doubt you have observed your wife's deterioration in the last few days," he continued. "This will unfortunately gather pace and of course we will do everything possible to keep your wife pain free and comfortable, but it will mean she will be heavily sedated and asleep most of the time. I really am most dreadfully sorry, Mr Jones. There is nothing more I can do. Can I suggest that perhaps you pop along to see Dr Powell yourself as I am sure he will be a great comfort to you at this terrible time. It is so important that you hold yourself together as much as possible and get your proper sleep, and so on."

As Dick's eyes brimmed with tears, Aunty Jo took over. "Don't worry, Doctor, I'll see they are alright. There's a little girl, five years old, as well as Joan's dad. He's sixty-eight and lost his wife a few weeks ago but I'll be looking after them."

They went and sat with Joan for about an hour. Dr Long had been right, she was sound asleep. As they left, the ward sister beckoned them into her office. "Dr Long has explained your wife's situation to me, Mr Jones. Please feel free to visit her at any time – ignore the usual rules about visiting hours." Dick managed somehow to say "Thank you."

When they arrived home at 9 o'clock, Jack had gone to bed. He would be up at 5.30 in the morning so it was nothing unusual. Dick and his sister sat either side of the range in the kitchen and talked well into the night. "You know, Barb," he said, "I am sure Joan knew last week that she was dying. When she told me she had to go into hospital for tests, she said that we'd just got to get on with it. I think she was telling *me* to get on with it, and on Sunday she took Mary up on to the hill – that was strange for her to go mooning about on a Sunday night. Another thing, a few years ago we had our photo taken at the County Show, just the two of us. This fellow popped out from behind a tent and snapped us. 'Only half a crown,' he said, 'I'll send you the prints next week.' I was just about to tell him to bugger off but Joan looked at me with them big blue eyes and said, 'Go on, Dick, give it to him.' I could never refuse her anything when she flashed them eyes, not that she's ever asked for much. Anyway, he did send the photo and I must admit it is a real beauty. He took us by surprise so it's all natural like. I noticed this morning that she's found it out over the weekend and put it into Mary's room, by her bed." He choked back the tears. "And on Monday," he continued, "she seemed to be drawing away from Mary a bit. Mary was in the orchard and although I've fenced the pond off really well, Joan still worried about her when she was out there playing. Well, on Monday she didn't seem too bothered. She'd washed her face and wiped her bottom for her and everything, but it was as though she was gritting herself to hand her over. What do you think about Mary going to see her, Barb?" he asked.

"What do you think?" Aunty Jo replied.

"I don't think it's a good idea, can't see the point somehow," Dick said.

"I totally agree," said Aunty Jo, "we'll never let Mary forget her mom, don't you worry about that, but it's the mom in the photo she must remember, not the one laying in Chesterton General."

"What about her dad?" asked Dick.

"The sooner, the better, Dick. I'd get it over with in the morning if I were you. We'll all rally round him and, my God, he's going to need that."

Dick took his sister's advice. The next morning, as soon as Jack came in from feeding the hens, Dick quietly told him that Joan was desperately ill and not expected to recover. "She could die in the next couple of weeks, Dad, but we've got to keep on going the best we can, for her sake and for Mary."

"My God, what have we done to deserve all this, what have we done?" was Jack's reply as he slumped into his chair, leaning slightly forward with his hands clenched between his knees. "I must go and see her tonight," he said.

"Dad, it's up to you. Barbara and me are going but she's hardly going to wake up apparently, so there's no point in upsetting yourself anymore than necessary – let's see how you feel later on."

Joan died on Wednesday April 26th, eight days after entering hospital, and just seven and a half weeks after her mother. Dick had told the Evans' family about the situation on the Friday morning, after his fateful meeting with Dr Long. Harry and Nancy Evans and George were stunned by the news. "If there's anything we can do," was repeated a dozen times. "I'll need a day or two off at some stage," Dick had said quietly.

"But of course," said Harry. "Whatever, Dick, please do what you want to round here – come and go as you please."

"I'll be better at work when I can," Dick continued. "My sister, Barbara, is with us for a while 'till things get sorted out. Jack's in a bad way, so soon after Rose, but between us we'll all pull through somehow."

The Evans' were undoubtedly shocked and were sympathetic towards their employee and his family who lived at the end of the drive. "Use the van whenever you like, Dick," they had said, but their compassion had its boundaries. Mrs Evans sent a big jam sponge over for them and a jar of homemade chutney, but did she go to see how Mary was faring, or to ask if she would like to go down and play with Elizabeth for a while? She did not. She certainly made a point of enquiring daily of Dick as to everyone's well-being, but with Aunty Jo now having to combine her professional duties with the household chores at the farm cottage, did she ever cross the threshold with words of comfort, or offers to fetch shopping, or sew, or clean, or sit with Mary? She did not. What the Evans' did was just about seemly, certainly no more.

Joan's funeral came and went. A quiet affair for a quiet family – a time of great pain and sorrow. Dick was living his daily life as if walking through a sea of treacle, and Jack hardly left his chair where faithful Hettie would lie quietly with her sleeping puppies, staring at him as if she knew of the anguish that was searing through his mind, and the anxiety and despair that washed over him in endless black waves. Aunty Jo bottled everything up but for the sake of everyone she kept going with not a break in her step. The house was cleaned, the meals were cooked, the washing and ironing was done as fast as she could get it off their backs, and little Mary, accepting that Mommy had gone to help the angels, was hugged and kissed and tapped and scolded, whenever and whatever the situation dictated.

On the Sunday after the funeral, Aunty Jo went to St Mark's morning service as was her habit. A prayer was said for the Jones' family and for Jack Berry. As she was leaving she saw Nancy Evans taking her leave of the vicar who was clasping her hand. Aunty Jo caught only snippets of their exchanges, "a terrible time for you all", "we are doing all we can to help, Vicar", "I am sure you are – they are fortunate to have people with sound Christian principles living so close." Aunty Jo had heard enough, writhing inside at such blatant hypocrisy, she hurried through the churchyard as fast as she could without breaking into a run, mounted her bike which she had left propped up against the wall near the lych gate, and peddled furiously back up the hill to Crest Farm Cottage. The Evans' overtook her in the Rover – they did not wave.

About a month after the funeral, Dick and Aunty Jo were sitting quietly either side of the range in the kitchen. Aunty Jo was darning one of Dick's socks, Jack had gone to bed at 9.30, his usual time, and Mary was peaceful in her infant slumbers. Dick had made them mugs of Ovaltine and he set one down beside his sister then, mug in hand, settled back into his chair.

Aunty Jo began, "Dick, we've got to have a talk. I've got such a lot of things to say, things to tell you. I was talking to Dr Powell last week about the situation here, what with my job and everything. There's no way I can leave here with things like they are. Now if you want me to leave it at that, for the time being, I will. I know you are still hurting like hell inside, and Jack's the same. He's lost the two most precious things in his whole life and things'll never be the same for him again, except that perhaps Mary, hopefully, will fill the dreadful emptiness you are both feeling. Anyhow, there's a whole lot of sorting out to do. The main thing is, I'm staying. If I don't, Dr Powell says the likelihood is that Mary would be taken into care by the authorities. I couldn't live with myself, couldn't let that happen, so that's that." She paused for a few seconds and took two or three sips from her mug.

Dick picked up on Aunty Jo's mood. "Barbara, I'm so grateful and so relieved but if you have got anything else on your mind, just carry on. It's probably what we both need and I'm not daft. I know things have got to be sorted, with your job and everything, so get it all off your chest, whatever's in your mind, get it all out."

"Well, first thing," said Aunty Jo, "you know when Dad died and we both finished up with about £200 each, and I had the house, well I put my money in the Post Office and I've never touched it. I always felt a bit uncomfortable about having the house all to myself. I know you said it was my home and that I had looked after Mom and Dad for twenty odd years, but I always felt you were entitled to something. Anyway, going back to the money in the Post Office, I am going to draw it out to buy a little car. George Baylis down at Ampleford Motors has got a green Morris Minor shooting brake, nice and sturdy it is. It's been his wife's runabout and there ain't a mark on it. It's £180 so I can well afford it, and Dr Powell says he'll arrange for the county to buy some petrol and help with the tax and insurance. I've still got my driving licence, through the Army, from the volunteer work I did in the war, and you can drive it as well, without keep borrowing that farm van and, quite honestly, at forty-one I can't keep biking for ever – going up and down that blasted hill will kill me. Now, going back to the house. I'm going to leave it, in a proper will like, to Mary. I've got no-one else and it'll put my mind at rest to know she'll have it one day. I'm determined not to sell it, Dick, just 'cos I'm living here. Mr Barker at the market auctioneers, you know, the one who deals with private property and that, says I can let it for ten shillings a week and, if I leave some furniture in it, sort of let it furnished. The way the law is, we could always repossess it for our own use if we need to. When you look back, it's marvellous how Mom and Dad brought us up, bought that house in Lower Street, and still managed to save a few hundred pounds. Dad only ever worked on the railway but do you remember how Mom did three cleaning jobs at one time when I was at college and you were still at school? She used to clean one house in the morning, one in the afternoon, and then go and clean at the school at 6 o'clock for two hours. No, I'll be damned if we'll ever sell that house after what she sacrificed to pay for it. The other thing is that I shall have to have the 'phone put in, Dick. Sometimes folks needs me quick but, there again, Dr Powell says I can claim expenses from the county for the calls, and it'll make life so much easier all round.

"Now, about the housekeeping and bills and everything. I'm going to carry on with my job so I feel I should put something in. I know there's no rent to pay with it being a tied cottage and all, but in my eyes you pay the rent with the sweat of your brow, so whatever work I do here with washing and cooking and everything will level that up. I think if we both put thirty shillings a week into a box, and ten shillings off Jack from his pension, that should take care of all the groceries, bread, meat and so on, but you'll have to give me another five shillings a week to put in another box for Mary's things. I'm determined to send her out nice, Dick, what with her going to school in September. Whatever rent I get for the house, I'm going to try and put in the Post Office. I'll gladly change it into a joint account if you like, and then if you've got a bit left over I can put it in at the same time. It'll either be for a rainy day, or for Mary one day. I'm sure we won't regret it. Lastly, Dick, 'cos I seem to have been going on for hours, we shall have to split one of the bedrooms upstairs. I can't stay in Mary's room forever. It won't be right for either of us, but I think you should leave Mary's room alone, and Jack's. I think your room should be made into two. It's plenty big enough but there's no hurry at the moment."

"Barbara, I don't know what to say," Dick replied. "You've hit me with so many things. First of all I've never had a problem with the house. I always thought you should have it, and what you've said about a will and everything is great with me. Mary's so lucky to have you as an Aunty, and I shall be making sure she knows that as she grows up. You can be certain of that! About the car, it's worried me stiff with you biking so much, and this hill and all, but I'm determined about one thing, Barb, we'll buy it between us. I never touched Dad's money either, and Joan was always so careful. We always managed to have a few shillings left over and she'd often put two or three quid in the bank on market days. So, no argument! I'll draw out whatever you want on Monday and we'll buy the car half and half. About the groceries and so on, I'll give you two pounds a week, not thirty shillings, but don't ask Jack for anything. He'll insist on you having something out of his pension but leave it to him. Believe me, I know him – that's the best way, just take what he offers. He's got a wooden box under the bed. He's never said anything to me but he told Joan. He's always been a tight so and so, never wasted a farthing, and he told Joan she'd have a shock if she knew how much was in it. Well, being a woman, she looked, didn't she, one day when he was out, and she reckoned there's about two hundred and fifty pounds in it. Believe me, Barb, when he's given you a bit of housekeeping, nearly all the rest will go into the box. Joan said something about a bank account once and he got a bit shirty, so she never mentioned it again. Joan said leave him to it. It gives him comfort somehow and, as she said, whatever's there would be hers and Mary's one day." He paused. "Barb, we're so lucky to have you. I don't know what would have happened if…"

Aunty Jo stopped him. "Listen, Dick, I'm just as lucky as the rest of you. Do you think that I liked living on my own? I've made the best of it these last few years, but it's been bloody lonely at times, I can tell you. I'd have loved to have got married and have kids but it never happened – no-one ever came along, no bloke ever looked at me twice to be honest. Mind you I've had one or two funny looks from other women but we won't go into that. They got short shrift I can tell you. So you see, Dick, to come here is just as good for me as it is for you. It's as though Him above has found something for me to do, and to be honest, although I loved Joan dearly, in my own way I'm loving doing her job. Do you understand that, Dick?"

"Of course I do," said Dick, realising that his sister was baring her soul as she had never done to anyone before.

"I know I can't completely take her mother's place," she continued, "and I'm making sure we talk about her every day, and that Joan's photographs are everywhere, but you might as well know, Dick, in the last two months I've come to love that little girl so much, she's number one for me now, Dick, top of the list in my book." Aunty Jo had never been one to show much emotion but Dick thought she wiped a solitary tear from her eye. Later, Dick cried himself quietly to sleep but his tears were not entirely tears of grief.

Things gradually began to return to normal at the farm cottage. Permission was sought from Harry Evans, and readily given, to split a bedroom into two. Dick was helped by Hans, an ex German POW who had come to work at the farm some three years before. He lived in an old caravan in the rickyard, was a popular man, and having married a local girl, had settled at Crest Farm. He was a more than adequate engineer with the tractors and implements, and a talented carpenter.

Aunty Jo, meanwhile, was striking up quite a friendship with Molly Perkins from down the lane. By the time she had reached Molly's patch, when she was still biking up the hill, she would have got off the bike and be pushing it for the last few hundred yards to the top. Whenever Molly spotted her, it would be, "Hello, Nurse, best come in and have a cup of tea and get your puff back." Molly had been so supportive to them all in several ways. It was she who looked after Mary on the day of Joan's funeral. In the weeks following, she showered them with big meat pies and cakes, and on numerous occasions she called at the cottage to see if there was anything she could do. She was a character was Molly, big and fat, with a bright red face that was topped with the thinnest, wispiest hair imaginable. Aunty Jo described her to Dick as being a bit rough but with a heart as big as St Mark's Church bell. "She's clean enough," she would say, "but I've never seen her yet when she wasn't sweating, and that little lad of hers, Billy, God only knows who his father is – she's never let on. He's nearly seven now and still walking round with a big rubber dummy in his mouth, ginger hair and more often than not, his pants full of poo. I remember delivering him. She had him so easy it wasn't true and I found her the next afternoon up the fields hoeing the strawberries. Honestly, Dick," she continued, "she's a real trooper and she's so funny, she gets all her words mixed up. She told me yesterday that the weather had been 'diabetical', and after all the rain we've had the brooks and ditches were all 'block-a-chock', and when I suggested to her that with Mary starting school soon we would be able to share taking Mary and Billy back and forth to Ampleford, she said, 'That's the way it should be with us country folk. We've got to help one another. You scratch your arse and I'll scratch mine, that's what I say, duck.'

"Honestly, Dick, I nearly killed myself laughing. How I kept a straight face I'll never know."

To everyone's great delight and pleasure, the Morris Minor arrived. Four weeks later, Aunty Jo heard a knock on the kitchen window as she washed the Sunday lunchtime crockery in the sink. It was Nancy Evans, with her daughter, Elizabeth. Aunty Jo had seen them through the window and whilst she busily dried her hands on her apron, she opened the back door. "Hello, Mrs Evans, you could have come to the front door, but never mind, come in," she said.

"No, it's alright, no need to disturb you, it's only a quick word," Nancy replied. She continued, "It's about the car, the green second-hand one. You see, for the last four weeks you've parked it permanently outside the front of the cottage. Now from our dining room window, we look straight through the orchard and out on to this cottage. It's such a pretty view, with all the roses and hollyhocks and everything. Well, all we can see now is the car, parked at the front dominating the picture somehow. I wonder if you'd mind bringing it down the drive and putting it into one of the cart sheds? Harry says it will be fine with him – that's all, really. The car will be quite safe and in the dry so I'll leave it at that." With that they were gone.

Aunty Jo shook with fury, her face whitened and she clenched her fists with rage. "Can you bloody well believe it?" she said, trying hard not to shout and bawl but with so much force in her voice that the words came spitting through her gritted teeth. "After all this family's gone through, the first and only bloody time she's come to the door and she's come to complain about the car offending her bloody view. The cow, the selfish cow, and that little girl stood there with her, there's something strange in her eyes, even at that age I can see it, such an air of superiority, bloody evil somehow." She became even angrier and louder. "How dare she come dictating to me, the nasty bitch. Who'd be missed more in this town, her or me? I'm telling you now they'm wrong uns. I don't know about the menfolk up at that farm but that Nancy and Elizabeth, they'm just horrible. Have you seen the way that Elizabeth rides her pony round the orchard and up and down the drive? Six hundred bloody acres she's got to ride it round, but no, she's got to flaunt it under our Mary's eyes ain't she. What'd it hurt her to come up the path and give our Mary a little go? Not on your bloody life – selfish, bleedin' hypocrites, that's what they am, and I'll tell you something else. That seed salesman's up there a lot ain't he? How often does a seed salesman have to call at a farm, for Christ's sake, and why's he always up there for two or three hours or more on a market day when Harry Evans is down in the market? I wasn't born yesterday, Dick, I didn't come in with the cows. You mark my words, just mark my words, the Lord works in funny ways at times, but they'll get their come-uppance one day. I just hope I'm about to see it, that's all. I just hope I'm still here to see it."

Aunty Jo left the car where it was. She pulled her old bike out of the shed and pedalled furiously down into Ampleford, where she set about cleaning and clearing the old family house in Lower Street. After some six hours, at 10 o'clock she biked all the way back, slumped exhausted into her chair, and calmed her shredded nerves with the help of several glasses of Jack's plum wine.

CHAPTER TWO

The market town of Ampleford, in the county of Mellshire, is on the banks of the River Mell. Travel south from the town and you will go past the John Bull Inn, an old coaching tavern. The bridge over the river leads you to four crossings – the signpost indicates Chesterton to the right, a left turn will take you towards the almost endless dalelands of the east, and straight ahead is the gradual climb to the summit of Crest Hill.

The journey out of the town in this direction embodies the beauty of rural England in all its finery: the willows that gently sway over the crystal waters of the fast running Mell, shallow at this point, the site of an ancient ford; the sturdy oaks that line the lower end of the lane that rises to become Crest Hill; the rolling water meadows, rich and fertile, that are the lower limits of Crest Farm; and as one slowly climbs the bank, the upper hill land, often bare and barren but with a wild beauty, stark and unbridled, in direct contrast to the quiet, rich greens of the lower land.

Molly Perkins' house and buildings stood on the left of the lane and were skirted, on the upper side, by a deep rutted track which was Molly's western boundary. All the land to the left of the track was Molly's, all the land to the right was Evans' land. The track snaked up the hill to Crest Pool, a twenty-five acre lake bounded on the southern side by the beautiful fells of Crest Farm. The lake was an area of outstanding beauty with an abundance of trees growing along its shore on the southern side. There were little beaches around the track's end and tall reed beds swayed like a vast, whispering blanket over much of its surface. The only access to the lake was up Molly's track, but apart from the occasional fisherman, bird watcher, and now and then a courting couple, the lake was rarely visited. The lake was a haven of wild life with badger setts nearby, otters thrived, and there was a multitude of bird life from the tiny reed warblers to the huge Canada geese that came to rest and breed every summer. Two streams drained from Crest Pool: one meandered its way through Molly's patch, bringing natural irrigation to her entire seventy acres; the other, to the western side of the track, was the main artery for more or less the whole of Crest Farm. It watered the middle ground, making it into fertile, arable land and rich cattle grazing meadows, then on down to nourish the sumptuous water meadows, before passing through a culvert beneath the road into the River Mell.

Molly's patch had been in her family for more than a century. Her grandfather and father had farmed it extensively and productively with cattle, pigs and poultry, as well as their market garden activities with fruit and vegetables. In recent years, Molly, realising the limits of her capabilities, had leased fifteen acres of water meadow to the Evans' for one hundred pounds per year. She also let them graze the twenty-five acres of upper land that reached up to the lake, but this was poorer land and she was quite happy for them to provide her with an ample supply of farmyard manure for her own thirty acres, in exchange for the grazing rights. Molly kept hardly any livestock now, just a little flock of bantams for their eggs, when she could find them, a pig to be killed every autumn to provide her with her own bacon throughout the winter, and three geese which she fattened up every year for Christmas – one for herself, and two to give away as gifts to Dr Powell and to Mr Lewis, the accountant who did her tax and things.

Molly lived solely for her land. Her entire life had been spent sowing and planting, hoeing and weeding, picking and selling her produce. She left the patch only twice weekly. Tuesdays would see her in Ampleford livestock market, where she would park her battered old van at the entrance to the stockyard and sell whatever she could from its back end. She was a character and she was popular. On Saturdays she was in the town market hall, selling her produce from the same stall her father and grandfather had occupied for decades. Molly wasn't short of money, in fact she was worth a nice bob or two. She never spent money on anything of any consequence – certainly holidays, clothes or make-up were a million miles from her thoughts, and she wasn't house-proud. Anyone who accepted her invitation to 'come on in and have a cup of tea' could not help but notice her struggle to find a cup with a handle on it, and of the eight chairs that surrounded the kitchen table, no two were a pair. Molly's whole life was her work in the fields. Only when the weather was so bad that she had to stop indoors would she do a bit of housework, otherwise it was seven days a week, sunrise to sunset, lovingly tending her patch. From April to October the house was a muckhole, never touched, but the fields and the crops were immaculate, and her bank balance was ample evidence of her graft.

Whilst all the farmers and local folk liked and respected Molly, she was, to some degree, a butt for their bawdy humour, particularly after the arrival of her baby, Billy. Her customers, especially the farmers, had always pulled her leg a bit. "Mornin' Moll," it would be.

"What you lookin' fer this mornin'?" she'd ask.

"Well, a naughty girl 'ud be nice, Moll. I'se got a fruity sort of feelin' in me bones somehow. Con yer suggest anythin' suitable?"

"Ther' ent much difference atween a naughty girl and a dirty ummun in my book," she'd cackle, throwing back her head in peals of raucous laughter revealing her gums, now the home of just two solitary molars, "an' if it's a dirty ummun you wants, they tells me they'm a tanner a jump down behind the picture house in Chesterton."

"Moll, you little rascal, you seems to know a lot about it. You ent bin makin' a few shillin' on the side I hope?"

"Certainly not, I'se always found it bloody ockward on me side anyroad," she'd shriek back.

After the birth of Billy there were many lewd conversations in the market bar, accompanied by much ribald chortling, but thankfully it was all behind Molly's back, well out of earshot. The local farmers divided roughly into two groups – those who went to market to do business and then went home, and those who went to market to do business and then get drunk. The latter group were the main protagonists of Molly's situation. Seated around a table in the market bar they were a motley crew, about twenty strong, mostly in their sixties and seventies – the young ones would have gone home to do the milking. They were a typical mix of tenant farmers, landowners and scarecrows. Their only journey down their farm drive was almost always to go to market, the exceptions being the odd point-to-point, wedding or funeral. There they would sit in their cowgowns, boots and gaiters, old flat caps, pork pie hats, and greasy trilbys, faces like roosters and bellies like beer barrels, discussing the weather and then the market prices, moving on to how badly off they all were and, as the session progressed, amidst arguments as to whose round it was next, they would engage in an earnest debate about who was going bankrupt and who was making a good fist of things. Inevitably, as the beer and whisky took over, the interchanges would descend to basement levels. "I'se jus' bin lookin' at that babby of Molly Perkins," one would say. "He's the spit out o' your bloody mouth, George, red hair an' all. Christ alive, you must a got pissed that night an' found yerself halfway up Crest Hill."

"An' finished up halfway up Molly Perkins," came a quick retort, amidst gales of smutty laughter.

"I'se never bin that pissed in me life I don't think," replied George Bailey, "not pissed enough to mount Molly anyroad. I reckons it 'ud be a back scuttlin' job, up agen' a wall like."

"Bloody hell, it'd atter be a soddin' strong wall," somebody said. "Anyroad up, it jus' gus ter show, any big fat ummun con get shagged if her waits long enough and finds a bloke pissed enough."

"And with a cock long enough to reach in Molly's case," said George.

"Come on, George, we all knows you'm hung like a bloody elephant. You fits the bill perfeck you duz, bloody own up like a mon."

And so it went on. Molly never divulged who had fathered her child. There was much conjecture about a family of gypsies who had helped her with the strawberry picking. The time fitted, but Molly went to her grave with her secret and Billy never became sufficiently mentally aware to bother. Meanwhile, Molly went relentlessly on with her daily chores and kept putting the money in the bank. An object of ridicule she may have been, something she half suspected, but the fact was that she could have bought and sold most of her tormentors twice over and she knew it.

Crest Farm was certainly very different to Molly's hobbledy-hoy of sprawling ramshackled buildings. With Molly's buildings not being used for livestock any more, she didn't see the sense in spending good money on maintenance beyond the basic absolute necessities. The sandstone barns, the timber sheds, the old pigsties and sheep pens were all full to brimming with the crates and boxes, punnets, baskets, nets and implements she needed for her market gardening activities. For this usage, a lack of the odd window pane, a tile or two off the roof, a creaking door, or a blocked drain, made little or no difference. "They ent fallin' down, an' if I spends a load of money on 'em I shan't grow one single more sprout or strawberry," Molly said. She made sure the house was given a lick of paint now and then, but the buildings were little short of derelict.

Not so at Crest Farm, where everything was as immaculate as farming activities would allow. There was never a quiet day at Crest Farm. The months from November to February, which were months of relative inactivity, were given over to repairs and renewals by the Evans brothers. When the weather allowed, fences were mended or replaced, areas of the yard resurfaced, doors and windows were repaired and refitted. You would never find a leaking roof or a blocked drain at Crest. Both the Evans brothers had grown up to become more than competent carpenters and bricklayers, and even the simpler plumbing and electrical tasks were not beyond them. Not for Harry and George the usual winter pursuits of their contemporaries – they did not hunt, fish or shoot. Apart from the odd Saturday point-to-point, their hobby was their farm, and it was a credit to them.

Crest Farm was a mixed farm, that is to say a wide cross section of agricultural activities were engaged upon. There was a milking herd of fine quality Friesian cows, some one hundred and forty strong. There was a flock of six hundred breeding ewes, which meant that after lambing there could be close on one thousand five hundred sheep up on the high ground. There were beef cattle fattened for the local market – these were the by-product of the dairy cows, being the calves from their matings with the magnificent red and white Hereford bull. Wherever possible, all the food for the animals was home grown. The Evans brothers grew their own barley, wheat and oats, and milled the home grown grain to feed the cattle, pigs and sheep. There was always ample straw for bedding, and hopefully enough hay for winter fodder. Of course they had their difficult years, years when the weather played havoc with their plans, when the harvest was poor, and the fodder was both short and of low quality. They had learnt as young boys from their father that farming is not a 'get rich quick' game. They had learnt that if you could only survive in the lean times, keep the soil in good heart, and keep things more or less level business wise, the good years would give more than enough to make progress, big enough surpluses of grain, fodder and hard cash, to successfully weather the next inevitable crisis when it came. Old Mr Evans had bought Crest Farm in the 1860s. It was two hundred acres of rich, fertile land, stretching away from the homestead in a northerly direction, all the way down to the River Mell. He had bought it with profits from his milling and merchant's business, firstly as a sound investment for his money, and secondly to satisfy the deep-seated yearning he had long harboured, a yearning to work the soil. He was a devout Christian and a relentless churchgoer. He both practised and instilled into his sons the ethics of worship and work. The Evans' were solid, sober, staid and successful. The old man's thrift and the continued careful nurturing of the family's assets by his sons had enabled them to easily gobble up four hundred acres of high fell land, to the south of the farm, when it came up for sale in the savage economic depression of the early 1930s. This trebled their acreage to six hundred and, although the land was mostly unfenced and of poorer quality than the northern land, it was perfect sheep ground, and they seized the opportunity to expand their flock and, at the same time, release the lower land to grow more crops and graze more cattle.

In addition to the cattle and sheep, there were also pigs and poultry. The logic was that it would be rare for all their operations to be failing at one time. If the sheep didn't make money, the pigs probably would. It was an integrated system that spread the risks. If the pigs were not profitable at least their manure was feeding the soil which grew the grass for the cattle and sheep. It would be very unusual if, at any one time, something was not earning high profits, whilst other things would be just nicely ticking over. The high level of stocking at Crest Farm demanded a sizeable workforce so, besides the brothers, there were always six full time men on the payroll. The Evans brothers were good people to work for and experienced no difficulty in finding good, local countrymen to employ. Usually the staff included a cowman, a shepherd, a tractor driver and three general labourers who fitted in where they were needed. The poultry were mostly looked after by the womenfolk. What had been started off by old Mr Evans as a few hens running round the yard to lay eggs for the house, had now grown into a flock of six hundred laying fowl, providing an important weekly income of ready cash all the year round.

As the flock had grown, old Mrs Evans had sought the help of Rose Berry to help her with the daily chores. Rose Berry received no pay for the help she gave Mrs Evans – she was quite content in the satisfaction of being a good neighbour, and to have free eggs for her kitchen, plus a nice boiling fowl now and then. Mrs Evans and Rose got along fine. They were friends and, although her sons were older than Joan, there was a special kind of bond between them, a bond that often exists between two mothers, a bond that allowed them to share the trials and tribulations of family life, and so, on the basis that a problem shared is a problem halved, they both drew mutual solace and comfort from each other's company.

When Mrs Evans passed away, Rose took on the care of the poultry on her own, with Jack helping her as much as possible. Inevitably, Joan was drawn in and, along with her dad, they continued with the care of the Crest flock. As Jack's age began to slow him down, the care of the poultry became an increasing part of his daily life. It was good for him – it kept him active and engaged him in something close to the soil, satisfied him and made him feel useful. Whilst he still worked with his collies, caring for the poultry was about the limit of his physical capabilities. Following the appalling events of March and April 1946, caring for the poultry helped to pull Jack across the terrible chasms of black despair and desolation that threatened to suck him down into the depths of mental oblivion.

One thing was certain, Nancy Evans was never going to help with the poultry, or anything else for that matter. Prior to his marriage in 1936, it had seemed that both Harry Evans and his brother would remain bachelors for all time. They were comfortably looked after by Miss Cummings, their housekeeper, who arrived at 8 o'clock each morning, seven days a week. Miss Cummings, a spinster in her mid-fifties, would prepare breakfast, scrub and clean the house, prepare a light 1 o'clock lunch, wash and iron their clothes, and leave a hot meal, in the form of a hearty casserole or a roast joint, for their evening meal. She baked cakes and bread, sewed and darned, and in the autumn made jams and chutney and bottled fruit. She was a diamond. No-one ever understood why Harry Evans took up with Nancy Wright. They had absolutely nothing in common. Nancy and her father had moved into a bungalow on the edge of Chesterton in the early 1930s. Dennis Wright had made a nice little nest egg from his painting and decorating business – Nancy described him as an 'interior designer'. He had lost his wife several years earlier, and with Nancy, the apple of his eye, being employed in the bank in Chesterton, a move into the country environment seemed sane and sensible. As an only child, Nancy had been spoiled by her doting father and was used to getting everything she wanted and having her own way. Nancy was pretty with natural blonde hair, a dinky little doll of a lady who was never short of male pursuers. She was always made up and dressed up to the nines. Harry Evans' eyes had first lit upon her at the bank, and when she started turning up at church on Sundays, his eyes were captivated by her dainty good looks and her carefree mannerisms. Their first significant contact was when Harry gave her a lift home after the Harvest Supper at St Mark's church hall. He dropped her off outside her home with no physical contact beyond the gentlemanly hand he offered to assist her from the car, but not before she had suggested they have a night out at the picture house in Chesterton on the following Saturday, and supper back at the bungalow afterwards. Harry had led a sheltered life as far as the opposite sex was concerned. He had never experienced anything quite like the clinging, melting warmth that draped beside him in the darkness of the Chesterton Plaza that evening. The first ardent kiss, and the so obvious smouldering availability of the pretty young girl in his arms, left him excited, beguiled and besotted. It was Harry's first peep into the world of sexual voracity. They were married less than six months later but, sadly, Harry was destined never to fully cope with Nancy's rampant, lustful demands.

Once Nancy had coaxed Harry Evans into her web, she had been determined to hang on to him. She saw the valuable land. As a bank clerk she had seen the money. She saw social position, elevation into a strata of society around which she had previously only fluttered, but there were many things she had not seen. Nancy had not seen the wet, stormy days on Crest Hill, when the mud and cow shit came traipsing into Crest Farm kitchen on the brothers' boots. She had not seen the sheep with maggots eating their flesh away, the mastitis that plagued the cows, and the calves limp with dysentery. She had never anticipated the muck spreading when the whole farm, including the house, would be reeking with the retching stench of pig shit. She never understood the motivation that took Harry from their bed at 5.30 a.m. on a biting winter morning, to wage a relentless battle against snow and ice in order to give his stock the care and attention they demanded. Nor did she understand the need, when wet weather threatened, to be labouring into the night after a sixteen hour day, in order to harvest the grain or the hay. Nancy was no farmer's wife, with her high heels and nylon stockings, her varnished nails, her coiffured blonde hair, and her face meticulously painted up by 9 o'clock every morning; in addition she was completely ignorant of everything and anything agricultural. Her presence at Crest Farm was unnatural and, to some extent, unkind. She was like an Eskimo in the jungle, completely and utterly out of place.

In Nancy's first few weeks at the farm, Miss Cummings found her hours cut quite substantially. Nancy took over all the cooking and, much to Miss Cummings' irritation, issued her with a daily list of cleaning and household chores that she expected her to complete.

Gradually, however, Nancy began to spend most of her days away from her new home. She seized on any excuse to drive off before 10 o'clock, and stayed away until late afternoon. She buried herself in her committee work and attended endless coffee mornings for the church or some charity or other. She spent hours on fruitless, unnecessary shopping expeditions, and needed only the flimsiest pretext on which to visit anyone who would make her a cup of tea and listen to her small talk. Within six months, Miss Cummings' hours were fully restored, and apart from cooking the occasional evening meal, Nancy had little domestic input. It had to be said that in some respects Nancy was a woman of great flair and good taste, and she took much delight in redecorating and recarpeting the old farmhouse. Her purchases of new furniture, pictures and porcelain to mix and blend with the valuable antiques that were there when she arrived, revealed her undoubted talent.

Secretly, Harry's brother George did not condone the upheaval; secretly, George did not like his new sister-in-law and her intrusion into their well-ordered lives. He loved his younger brother dearly and had no intention of making his feelings known. He knew how terribly hurt Harry would be and, even more significantly, the possibility of damaging their successful business partnership was a prospect he could never consider. George retired quietly to his room most evenings to listen to his wireless and read his books, quite content to leave Harry and Nancy to each other's company. George was comfortable in the knowledge that by birthright half the farm, lock stock and barrel, would always be his.

Nancy kept up the charade of dutiful, doting housewife for two and a half years. She accompanied Harry to the Farmers' Union dinners, attended church and filled his bed but the truth was, she was deeply unhappy. Certainly she revelled in the social elevation her marriage had given her. The Evans' family had always been highly respected and could loosely be bracketed as 'county folk'. Nancy had carried herself admirably, with great charm and dignity when the occasion demanded but, nevertheless, nothing could alter the facts that firstly she was a square peg in a round hole at Crest Farm, and secondly that Harry Evans had never once scratched beyond the surface of the deep passions that pounded like tidal waves through her body.

In the autumn of 1939, Nancy was bracing herself to leave. She spent two or three weeks quietly, cynically gathering together details of bank accounts, stock valuations and balance sheets, in readiness for a divorce wrangle. Gradually, however, another devastating realisation was dawning on her – she was pregnant. Nancy bided her time, and a visit to Dr Powell some three weeks later confirmed what, by now, she was already sure of.

"Congratulations, Mrs Evans," the doctor said. "Harry will be as proud as punch I'll wager – an heir to the Evans' fortunes, someone to leave his money to and all that. I'm sure everything will be alright. You need have no worries, you're a healthy, fit young woman. It must have been a bit lonely for you at times up on that hill but you'll have plenty to think about now with a little one coming, and you'll certainly have plenty to do when it comes. Come and see me again in about three months and we'll keep an eye on you."

"I shall be going into a private nursing home or something when the time comes," Nancy replied. "Harry will only want the best of everything for me and the baby, I'm sure."

"Be that as it may," the doctor continued, "but I'll look after you in the meantime. We're quite happy to do the spade work and let someone else take all the glory. Please give my best regards to Harry and his brother, and don't forget to make an appointment to see me in about three months."

Nancy's plans to leave Harry had evaporated like mist on a midsummer morning. She'd had thoughts of going back to her father's bungalow, securing a hefty settlement and suing Harry for divorce on the grounds of his unreasonable behaviour, denial of conjugal rights and so on, and then casting her net around for a more suitable companion. Being pregnant, she realised she might be on sticky ground now. Nancy had yearned for the bright lights, for the shops and cinemas, the dance halls and the theatres. Harry's idea of giving her a day out was a visit to an agricultural show or ploughing match, but for now Nancy had to get on with it. She realised that, with a small child in tow, she was not going to be a very attractive proposition to another man. For once in her life she was not getting what she wanted, not for the time being anyway.

Harry was tickled pink with the news. He had long ago sensed his wife's sullen moods, her difficulties in coming to terms with country life, and her restless hankering to be anywhere else but home at the farm. A baby would, he was sure, settle her down and give her a purpose. He indulged her every whim, including a booking into a nearby private maternity hospital, the very best and most expensive within striking distance.

Baby Elizabeth was born on January 26th, 1940. Nothing could diminish Harry's exuberant delight at the birth of his daughter, and Nancy surprised everyone with the genuine depth of her maternal instincts. She quickly demonstrated that little Elizabeth was the best thing that had ever happened to her, and for the next few years her devotion to her little daughter was total. There was no denying that Nancy had love by the bucketful to offer.

Unfortunately, she had not previously found a suitable recipient, certainly not in Harry Evans. In spite of the fact that in Elizabeth, Nancy had found someone on whom she could lavish her surplus affection, she was still not completely fulfilled. Harry's lovemaking remained shallow, dutiful and brief, a job quickly performed and then to sleep. After five years Nancy's deep-seated frustrations began to resurface, and then two fateful circumstances coincided in her life. Elizabeth started school at Belmont House, a small private establishment for about sixty pupils, the sons and daughters of the well off, and Gerald de Beau called at the farm selling seeds.

Gerald de Beau was an ex RAF navigator who had been invalided out of the Air Force after being shot down over the English Channel in 1941. He had enjoyed a distinguished, unblemished career in the service of his country, having been rewarded with the DFC before his untimely discharge. Gerald had bobbed about in the water for eighteen hours before being rescued, saved only by his Mae West. He was deeply unconscious when the Royal Navy hauled him aboard a patrol boat. Following a long and painful recovery from exposure, trauma and multiple fractures, including both legs and his collarbone, the RAF offered him the choice of a desk job or an honourable discharge. He chose the latter. He didn't fancy being involved with aeroplanes unless he was flying them. For Gerald, the exhilaration of the skies was irreplaceable – he didn't fancy being desk-bound.

Gerald had quickly landed a job as an area salesman for Hawkins and Bright, seedsmen. He had to cover an entire county, taking care of the needs of some two hundred farmers, and whilst he certainly did not consider this to be a job for the rest of his life, he was grateful to be on the move, meeting people and spending most of his time in the open air. Gerald was a popular man with both the farmers and their wives. With his pleasant, blokey personality and his inexhaustible store of smutty stories, the farmers found a man they could easily identify with. His dark good looks, deep blue eyes, immaculate grooming and impeccable manners made him an instant hit with most of the ladies. There were the odd one or two who found the MG car, his cravat, the 'what ho's' and 'old boys' that he employed constantly in his conversations, slightly oily, a bit spivvy perhaps, but there was no denying he had charm and charisma by the bucketful.

He breezed into Crest Farm one Monday morning in September 1945. The men were all out at work and the door was answered by Miss Cummings. "If you'll just wait a moment, I'll get Mrs Evans," she said. "Please stand inside." Nancy walked into the kitchen and extended her right hand, expecting a firm handshake of introduction. Instead, Gerald's hands took her fingers so lightly and lifted them delicately to his lips where he brushed them with the briefest of kisses.

"Gerald de Beau, ma'am, charmed and privileged to make your acquaintance," he drooled. He explained to Nancy who he was and the reason for his visit. He enquired when it would be convenient to come back and speak to Harry. His speech was eloquent – he used the words of a well-educated man and Nancy was utterly captivated. She cursed herself as he sped from the yard. Why hadn't she at least offered him a cup of tea? The presence of this divine human being had turned her into a trembling teenager but she took comfort in the fact that he had said he would come back very soon. She couldn't wait!

Gerald made an evening telephone call to Harry Evans and arranged to call on the following Saturday morning. This time, Nancy made sure he stayed for tea. She settled him into the comfort of the farmhouse lounge, brought out the best china and chocolate biscuits, before calling Harry from the yard. Gerald's experience as a navigator in the RAF had taught him that in spite of all the technology at his disposal, his training, the mathematics and geometry involved and, above all, the radar screen, basic human instinct played a major part in the success of the missions he undertook. Gerald's instincts were still razor sharp except that in civilian life his quarry was different. Gerald was a rake and could sniff out a bit of skirt a mile off. Along with a whisky and soda, there was nothing he relished more. It took him about ten seconds to lock on to Nancy's blatant signals. He was certainly receiving her, loud and clear – the fluttering eyelashes, the salacious glances, the wiggle in her hips, the persistent eye contact, and much more. He deliberately allowed one of his catalogues and price lists to slide behind the cushion of the big chair he was occupying, an old trick he had used before. He needed a plausible excuse to come visiting again. 'Whizz bang,' he thought as he roared off down the drive, his business with Harry completed. 'If she had been wearing a badge with "shag me" on it she couldn't have made it much clearer, whacko and zippedy doo dah.' Life was looking up.

Where matters of the flesh were concerned, Gerald had learnt not to let the grass grow under his feet – strike while the iron is hot was his motto. "If I don't satisfy her needs someone else will," he reasoned. The telephone duly rang at Crest Farm at 10.30 on Sunday morning. The men were busy in the yard, leaving Nancy and Elizabeth alone in the house.

"Hello, Mrs Evans." Gerald's plummy tones came dripping down the line. "Awfully sorry to bother you on Sunday morning but I seem to have mislaid some documents that are important to my work. It's a long shot, but I wonder if perhaps they may have slipped from their folder. I last recall using it yesterday when talking to your husband in the lounge."

"Please don't apologise," Nancy replied. "They haven't come to light, but if you will hang on for a moment, I'll go and take a look. It won't take a moment."

"I'll hang on for as long as it takes," was Gerald's reply. "Please don't put yourself to a lot of trouble."

"You're in luck," squeaked Nancy excitedly, less than a minute later, "they had slipped behind a cushion. Are you desperate for them? I could post them to your office later today if it helps."

"No, no," insisted Gerald, "I couldn't possibly put you to that trouble. It's just occurred to me, I shall be passing the farm on Tuesday about midday, just a matter of scooting down the old drive there and I can collect them, if that's convenient, of course."

"Yes, no problem," Nancy assured him.

"See you on Tuesday then," Gerald continued. "What a spiffing bonus to see you again so soon, and so unexpectedly. Bye for now." Nancy clutched the seed catalogue closely to her bosom. What a piece of luck – fate had taken over and Harry would be away at market, too.

"That Gerald, whatever his name is, 'phoned earlier," Nancy said to Harry when he returned for lunch. "He left a catalogue here yesterday by mistake and is going to pick it up one day next week, when he's in the area."

"Oh, right. Good, that's alright then. Seemed like a nice chap, bit smarmy somehow, but plenty about him," he replied, and dismissed the matter from his mind, a mind that was full to brimming with farming matters.

Nancy's demeanour took on a refreshed, cheerful flavour during that weekend. There was a new bounce in her step as she moved about the farmhouse. She was more tolerant with Elizabeth than usual, and took great delight in placing several vases of carefully arranged flowers in the hall and lounge. Even church on Sunday morning, which she usually found such an interminable drag, she took in her newfound light-hearted stride.

Tuesday came quickly. Nancy drove Elizabeth to school, stopped off in Ampleford to do some shopping, arriving back at Crest Farm at 10.30 a.m., just as Harry and George were leaving for market. Dick had left in the lorry two hours before, with forty plump sheep and fifteen porker pigs to be auctioned to the local butchers at midday, at which hour Gerald de Beau drove into the farmyard dead on cue.

"Please, do come in," enthused Nancy. "I have your papers in the lounge for you. Would you like a cup of tea or coffee perhaps?"

"Coffee would be lovely, so kind of you," Gerald replied, as Nancy ushered him gently into the lounge, after placing the kettle on the stove in the kitchen. Gerald was settling comfortably into an armchair when his eye lighted on a bottle of White Horse Scotch Whisky on the sideboard. "Mrs Evans," he began.

"Please, please call me Nancy," she interrupted as, for the second time, the chocolate biscuits were produced.

"Nancy, dear, you really are most uncommonly hospitable," Gerald continued. "Do you know, at this hour I am usually stood at some market bar nursing a Scotch and soda. This is much more civilised."

"Oh, how awful of me," Nancy groaned, "you don't have to have coffee. Please let me get you a proper drink. I can certainly fix you a whisky and soda if you prefer."

"No, no, I really wasn't, er, trying to prompt you," Gerald stuttered. "The coffee will be fine, honestly."

"I insist," said Nancy as she hurried to the kitchen to take the kettle off the stove, shouting back to him, "In fact, I will join you. What a lovely idea."

To say that Gerald was now in his element would have been a massive understatement. Like the cows that cropped contentedly on the late autumn grass, or the geese that floated serenely across the farm pool, he was utterly at ease with his environment. Gerald was indulging himself in something he knew he was good at. He had learnt years ago that an important element in the art of seduction was not to talk about himself. He gently questioned Nancy about her life, her family background, her feelings about her activities as a farmer's wife, and her thoughts for Elizabeth. He was particularly interested in the fact that she was a regular churchgoer and a great lover of classical music.

As the whisky gently melted Nancy's inhibitions, she began to respond and warm to Gerald's interest in her circumstances, and his willingness to listen with such obvious sympathy. Above all, for the first time in many years, she was talking to a man with whom she felt compatible and, although he was little more than a stranger, she was revealing some of her innermost feelings.

"Do you know," she said, "there have been times when this farm has seemed like a huge black hole that was slowly devouring me. I gave up years ago on the idea of helping outside. I tried to help them bring the sheep down off the fells one year, and no matter where I stood I seemed to be in the wrong place. Harry and the men spent most of the time bawling and shouting to me to move to a different position, but by the time I got there I was in the wrong place again." She managed a sardonic smile and continued, "It has never been suggested that I should go outside and help again. Makes one feel a bit of a fraud somehow. I mean, I am a farmer's wife but a bit useless really. It's not as though I haven't tried. It's difficult to believe that I've been up here for eight years, and I often wonder whether I would have lasted had Elizabeth not come along, but there you go – conjecture – I'm certainly not leading a life that I was cut out for."

Gerald interjected only occasionally and briefly. "You poor lamb", "how beastly for you", and "how on earth have you coped", dripped softly from his lips at appropriate moments.

Their conversation meandered on for more than two hours. They talked about virtually everything under the sun, from music to war, from holidays to fashion, with Gerald allowing Nancy most of the input, saying just enough to motivate her loquacity. Eventually, at about twenty minutes past two, Nancy's flow subsided. "Have you seen the time? I don't believe it, I have to pick Elizabeth up at 3 o'clock," she gasped as she rose to her feet.

"Oh dear, I've outstayed my welcome," Gerald replied.

"No, no, really, it's been absolutely lovely talking to you. I've enjoyed every minute. I do hope it won't be months and months before we see you again," Nancy pleaded.

"Look, I'll tell you what," said Gerald, "I've got a lovely gramophone down in the cottage and there's the collection of Mahler recordings I mentioned." Gerald was referring to the coincidence that had surfaced during their conversation – they both loved the music of Gustav Mahler. He continued, "Would it be too embarrassing for you to call down one day perhaps?" Gerald's cottage overlooked the river on the outskirts of Ampleford. "I fully understand that you might feel a bit compromised, but I do assure you that the invitation is totally without any devious motive."

For the first time Nancy was a little cautious. She paused for a few seconds, needing to weigh up the implications in spite of the fact that Gerald's invitation had set her heart fluttering wildly. "It sounds divine. Of course I will come." She could hardly believe what she was saying. Her words came out with a breathless excitement she could barely conceal. "I can't tell you exactly when I can come. Could I ring you on Saturday evening perhaps? Harry's off to a meeting." Already her mind was moving towards a road that was signposted 'deceit and betrayal'.

"Yes, of course," Gerald said, "don't worry unduly if you change your mind. Please don't feel under any obligation but it would be rather spiffing. Till Saturday then." He strode quickly across the yard, having gently shaken her hand and kissed her lightly on the cheek.

Harry Evans' mind, as always, was crammed with farming matters every waking hour of every single day – buying and selling stock, organising the men, planning their husbandry for the days ahead, their activities for the next few weeks, and the policies for the coming year. In spite of this single-mindedness, even he had taken on board Nancy's change of mood and he was pleased. Elizabeth starting school and Nancy's involvement with all the other mothers was the source of her 'joie de vivre', he reasoned – long may it continue.

On Saturday evening Nancy waited for nearly an hour after Harry's departure to his National Farmers' Union meeting. George Evans had returned from his last walk round the yards and buildings. Casting a keen eye across the calves and pigs and the bigger cattle in the fattening pens, all had been content, and no signs of any in distress with pending illness. He had now retired to his room carrying a tray with cocoa and biscuits. "I'm going up now then," were his parting words. As ever, George always listened to the Saturday night play before getting into bed at about 10 o'clock, and Nancy could hear the muffled tones of his wireless as she poured herself a Scotch and soda. Content that she was now in blissful isolation, she sipped her drink and picked up the 'phone. As she dialled Gerald's number she was vividly aware that by making this 'phone call, she could be changing her life forever.

Nancy and Gerald exchanged their normal pleasantries – both had enjoyed a busy week, both had enjoyed Tuesday enormously. After five minutes or so of idle chatter, Nancy said, "About your invitation to the cottage, I'd love to come but it won't be for a couple of weeks. Elizabeth's on half term holiday next week which constrains me somewhat. She goes back the week after, and on Thursdays she stays at school until 5 o'clock for extra music and dancing which she loves. If it's alright with you, I could pop along and have a cup of tea about half past two. I usually go shopping in the town on Thursdays anyway so it will suit me perfectly."

Gerald welcomed her suggestion warmly. "That's wonderful," he said, "it seems like a lifetime until next Thursday week. I shall count the hours." They continued to chatter for another ten minutes, then following exchanges of "take care of yourself", and "roll on Thursday week", Nancy hung up.

Nancy went shopping on the appointed Thursday as arranged. She made a few hasty purchases from the grocers, some items from Timothy White's, the chemists, and then into Woolworth's for some sweets for Elizabeth. She returned with her purchases to her car which she had parked discreetly behind the public toilets on the market car park. Carefully re-locking it, she started to walk the half mile or so to the outskirts of town, where Gerald's cottage overlooked the River Mell. She had taken little notice of the property previously, a tall privet hedge hiding all but the roof from view. It was set back from the road with the river snaking its way through the meadows on the other side of the road. The cottage enjoyed relative isolation – next door was a hundred yards away, with a neat little orchard and vegetable garden between them. Nancy admired the pretty garden with its old staddle stones either side of the path and an old millstone, covered with lichen, set up as a bird bath.

Gerald had seen her coming along the path and was all smiles as he helped her remove her coat and draped it carefully across a chair in the little hallway. She placed her handbag on the same chair. "Please come into the parlour," he said. "I will soon make you a nice, hot cup of tea." He had sensed that she was slightly cold, although she had not complained. "Come and sit by the fire," he continued, as he rustled the fire in the grate with a large iron poker, and placed timber logs on the embers.

Nancy's eyes were soon telling her that this was a bachelor's house, lacking feminine tastes and a woman's touch. Gerald came in with the tea on a tray, best china teapot, milk jug, cups and saucers and silver teaspoons. "I'll let you pour," he said as he placed the tray on a small antique table in front of the now blazing fire, and seated himself at the fireside opposite Nancy. "Now, isn't this just cosy, what?" he said as he started to sip his tea.

"This is a lovely cottage," Nancy said, "all these wonderful oak beams, the inglenook and the lattice windows, it's quite charming." Nancy had spotted some old family photographs in stand up frames on the sideboard, and a portrait of Gerald in full flying kit about to climb into an aircraft. "Oh, you must tell me about these people," Nancy said as she moved across the room. "I know so little about you."

"Well," said Gerald, "the only ones that are relevant are these two of Mother and Father. All the others are distant relatives from years ago, Mother's aunts and great aunts and so on. There seemed to be millions of them. I brought the old pictures from home when Ma and Pa passed on. I couldn't bring myself to chuck them out. As you can see, Father was a military man – Colonel in the Indian army, the British Raj, and all that. They moved out there soon after they were married. I was born out there and attended the English school for the sons of officers before coming back to Cranwell when I was seventeen. Mother and Father were out there for twenty-three years. He was discharged when he was fifty with a super pension, and Mother had inherited a handsome sum from her family, so they were extremely comfortable to say the least. Problem was, coming home killed them both in less than four years. Mother was always a bit sickly, caught everything going, and the change of climate, after so long in India, was a massive shock to her system. Also in India, of course, she was waited on hand and foot. There were servants for literally everything, but it isn't like that over here and she simply could not adjust. She died from pneumonia following a bout of influenza but would probably have lived another twenty-five years if she had stayed in India. Dad had similar problems but his inability to cope with civilian life was the main thing. He joined an ex-army officers' club soon after mother died and practically lived there. He could get a meal there which was nice for him but, unfortunately, he could also get an unlimited supply of Scotch. He drank himself to death – liver packed up – a bottle and a half a day, they told me, in his last year. So that's it really. I couldn't live in London so I sold everything, put the loot in the bank and got on with life in the Air Force, a twenty-seven-year-old orphan. When I copped my packet over the channel I was discharged, of course, so I drew some money from the pot and bought this. I like it. I liked where it was and it suits the job. I don't have to do this job, Nancy. I am a man of independent means as it were, and I don't intend to do it forever. At the moment it's convenient, it pays a few bills and keeps me out of mischief. I've actually got a good business idea, I think, and I'll tell you about it one day, but not today."

"Tell me about this picture of you and this lovely young girl," Nancy asked. She was completely fascinated by Gerald's story.

"Oh, we were engaged. Her name was Angela and she was a nurse at the military hospital where I spent three months after I ditched. Easiest thing in the world to fall in love with your nurse, and I proved it. She volunteered for ambulance work in the East End, the blitz and all that, and was helping to pull live victims from the basements of some bombed houses when the bloody lot fell on top of them. The bloody roof fell in, killed them all, bloody war, bloody war!"

Nancy reached out to clasp Gerald's hand. She pulled him gently towards her and kissed him softly and gently on the lips, a few brief seconds of compassion, sympathy and understanding. As they parted he replaced the photograph on the table. "No good looking back," he said, "today and tomorrow are what counts, yesterday's gone. Nancy," he paused, "we're going to be friends aren't we? I mean special friends. We'll look out for each other as it were. Would you like that?"

"Oh, yes, I would love that," was her simple reply. Gerald's story was searing through her mind. Beneath all that macho front he was something else, a lonely man who hadn't yet found a new niche, a new role to take the place of the Air Force, a man who had been dealt two savage blows, blows that would have devastated most men forever, and yet here he was, 'jack the lad', and fighting back. Oh, she would love to be his special friend, more than anything in the world.

The afternoon passed quickly, the Mahler went unplayed – they had talked so much. "What about next Thursday?" Gerald inquired.

"No problem as far as I can tell," Nancy replied. As he helped her on with her coat, he gently lifted her soft blonde curls from beneath her collar and kissed her gently on the lips.

"That's twice," he said, "and counting." She tripped off into the darkening street to retrieve her car and fetch Elizabeth from school.

Nancy busied herself through the following week, often finding herself daydreaming, mooning round the house with her mind a million miles away or, perhaps, just a short mile away at the riverside cottage. She dreamt of life at Gerald's side as his partner, as his wife. She pictured the cottage as it would be with her influence and she yearned for his touch, for the thrill of physical contact. She was besotted – she was in love.

The week soon passed, and on Thursday Nancy retraced her path to Gerald's cottage. This week was similar to the last except that the Mahler was played, the fourth movement of the fifth symphony, dreamy, wistful and evocative, music that was overflowing with subdued emotion and romance. Gerald took her into the garden at the rear of the cottage, where there was quite a substantial sandstone building which had been an old stable block. Inside, he revealed a rusty, dilapidated seed drill, a hay rake and an ancient grass mower, all in similar condition. "My business idea," he explained. "The countryside is heaving with old, broken-down implements, sometimes hidden from view beneath brambles and nettle beds, and I am going to rebuild and repair them. Get rid of the rust, paint them and put them back into full working order. These old bits of scrap can be bought for a song, and often people are just glad for someone to remove them. Farm sales are a rich picking ground, the seed drill there cost five shillings. It cost more to get it moved down here, ten shillings actually, but a new seed drill would cost one hundred and fifteen pounds. Two weeks' work by a good mechanic, say fifteen pounds per week, will restore that as good as new, total cost just over thirty pounds. I reckon with the way farming is, following the depression and the war and everything, that seed drill would be bloody attractive to a lot of them at fifty pounds, less than half the price of new. 'De Beau's Rebuilds', that's what I think I will call the company, or maybe 'G.D.B. Rebuilds Ltd'. I'll think about it. My slogans will be, 'Everything Less Than Half Price', and 'Remember Every Machine You Use is a Used Machine'. What do you think, Nancy?"

"I don't know. You would never find old scrap machines like that at Crest Farm, I can tell you," Nancy replied. "Harry and George have their own workshop and do all their own repairs."

"Look," said Gerald, "Crest Farm and the Evans brothers is not the norm, believe me. You would go fifty miles and not see another set up like theirs. In my travels over the last few months I could have picked up fifty machines like these for an outlay of probably less than a hundred pounds. Anyway, I am on the lookout for a mechanic. I'll fund the refurbishment of these three and advertise them, test the water as it were, but I'm certain I'm on to something. The thing is I can buy the scrap implements whilst I'm selling the seeds, for a little while anyway. That way, if it doesn't work, I've still got my job."

Nancy was fascinated. "It all sounds quite plausible," she said. "I do wish you all the luck in the world, and if it really takes off and you need office staff, do think of me."

"I never stop thinking of you," Gerald whispered, as he shepherded her back into the cottage. More tea was drunk.

"Play that wonderful Mahler again," Nancy pleaded. There was more conversation and as Nancy left, they kissed lingeringly, his arms round her waist, hers round his neck.

"Next week?" he queried.

"Try keeping me away," she murmured.

Throughout the following week Gerald thought often about Nancy. He had to concede to himself that their relationship was beginning to mean more to him than he had either anticipated, or intended. He had only ever once thought he was in love – with his beloved Angela. After the searing pain of her death, he had vowed that never again would he allow his emotions to become so deeply involved, so committed. Why then, he asked himself, was he living each week eagerly anticipating Thursdays? What was it about this perky little farmer's wife that made her different to any previous target for his lust? 'Christ,' he thought, 'I must be slipping – three dates already and mission still unaccomplished.' Gerald would normally have expected full servicing to have been attained by now, indeed long since, and yet somehow he didn't mind. Certainly, physically, he still found Nancy deliciously attractive. He ached for her. He practically salivated at the thought of her tight, round bottom, her silky legs and those bouncy little breasts, but there was something else. She was certainly different to Angela. Nancy, he rightly suspected, had been spoilt and was perhaps somewhat selfish. Angela had been none of those things. In spite of these misgivings, Gerald admitted to himself that he felt wonderfully comfortable in her company. She was a lovely companion with whom he could talk on almost any subject, and receive sensible, compatible responses. He realised that she genuinely was becoming a very special friend, accepting that the pleasures of physical union were not now the entire landscape of their relationship.

As Nancy drove down Crest Hill on the following Thursday lunchtime, it was raining steadily. There were pools collecting on the surface of the lane as she approached the bridge across the river. She parked her car as usual, and returned some twenty minutes later with her bits and pieces of token shopping. By now the wet, grey November weather was getting worse. Although it was barely half past one, the light was awful and the sky was a mass of black clouds whipped along on the gathering wind. Nancy fastened her coat up to the top button, raised her umbrella, and started her usual walk to Gerald's cottage. She had covered no more than two hundred yards when the heavens opened, and for the next ten minutes she was exposed to a deluge the like of which she had never previously experienced. The wind gusted to gale force, wrecking her umbrella and rendering it totally useless. The rain fell in dense clouds, hitting her horizontally. Within a brief minute or two her coat was waterlogged, her hair was lank and dripping, and her vision impaired by the rainwater that flooded her eyes. Had she jumped into the nearby river, she would not have emerged any wetter. Every square inch of every garment she stood up in was saturated. Gerald was appalled at the sight that greeted him when he opened the cottage door. The extreme physical exertions of the previous ten minutes had left Nancy in great distress and she was unable to speak, her teeth chattering incessantly. Within seconds of entering the cottage, her body had taken on a continuous, uncontrollable tremor.

Gerald unbuttoned her coat, removed it and held her bedraggled little body close for a few moments, quickly realising just how drenched and cold she was. "Right," he said, "just follow me," gently reaching for her hand. She followed him obediently into the hall and up the oak stairs to the landing on the first floor. He opened one of several doors that led off the landing to reveal a spacious bathroom. Gerald proceeded to fit the plug into the drain of the large white bath and filled it with hot water and soap flakes. Nancy was still shaking uncontrollably as he left her, saying, "Straight into that now, you'll soon thaw out. There's loads of towels in that cupboard, and use my bathrobe when you've finished. I'll get some hot coffee going and I'll sort out a tot of something. We'll soon have you warmed up and then we can set about getting those clothes dry. Now, straight into that hot water as soon as my back's turned, and stay there until you stop shivering." He closed the bathroom door and went downstairs to prepare the coffee.

Nancy quickly peeled off her soaking garments, stepping delicately out of her sodden knickers and into the welcoming warmth of the soapy water. Relief was almost instant and within a minute she had stopped shaking and chattering. Her previously numbed limbs began to glow. Nancy lay back in the soapy paradise and felt the heat coursing through her grateful body. The vicious, cold, lashing rainwater which had reduced her to a shaking, gibbering wreck, had been replaced by the caressing bath water that was rapidly restoring her to normality.

"You alright?" Gerald had inquired after about ten minutes.

"Yes, yes, wonderful, thanks. This is just wonderful, I'll be down soon," she shouted back. Soon she was curled up beside the crackling log fire in the parlour, with Gerald's bathrobe wrapped tightly around her glowing body. The flames licked and snaked up into the chimney as she took tiny sips of the hot coffee and brandy that Gerald had prepared. They were strangely silent. Conversation, for once, did not flow. Mahler, Gerald's business plans, the war and everything else seemed suddenly of no consequence. Gerald was acutely aware of her state of undress and Nancy, with converse curiosity, wondered if she was affecting him. In truth both were seething with excitement.

"Your clothes," Gerald murmured, "there's a gas fire in my bedroom so we can put them on the clothes horse in front of that to dry."

"Perfect," she replied.

They went back up the stairs to Gerald's bedroom where the gas fire was already on, giving the room a welcoming feel. Gerald fetched a wooden clothes horse from a nearby room and Nancy proceeded to carefully drape her various items of clothing along it. Both uttered not a sound as she turned towards the door to leave the room, but Gerald did not turn – they were left face to face. He leant towards her and gently clasped her pretty face, crowned with still damp curls, and kissed her firmly on the lips. Nancy's response was instant and positive. As she wrapped her arms around Gerald's shoulders, the bathrobe parted exposing her naked breasts. Her lips were slightly open, receiving Gerald's kiss with moist eagerness, whilst her body melted warmly into his arms. Gerald slid his arm inside the robe, firstly behind her back to gently stroke between her shoulders, then downwards to softly caress the firm cheeks of her bottom. Whilst still locked in this passionate embrace, they moved gradually towards the bed. As Nancy fell gently backwards on to the eiderdown, Gerald's bathrobe fell from her shoulders, leaving her naked. Gerald was fumbling to remove his tie, his pullover and his shirt. Gradually garment after garment was shed whilst they continued to explore each other's body. Eventually both were naked. For the next ten minutes they made wanton, carefree love, releasing a million effervescent bubbles of sexual pleasure to burst across their beings, to moans and groans of satisfying delight. The years of stifled libido Nancy had suffered came surging through the floodgates of her orgasm. Eventually they lay back, their naked bodies embracing, their lips still kissing.

As their pleasure peaks began to diminish they eventually fell apart, their desires sated, their bodies exhausted from the focussed efforts of their lust. Never before had Gerald experienced such natural, easy harmony. Here was a partner whose performance was so sympathetic to his gentle cajoling and who responded with such precision to his skilful directions. For Nancy, at last, at long long last, the depths of her needs and yearnings had been plumbed – Nancy had tasted nectar, Nancy had been to paradise, nothing less would ever do again.

Nancy suddenly rocketed from the bed. She had just heard the church clock striking five. "Oh, my God," she shrieked, "the time – I should be picking Elizabeth up, *now!*"

"Stop worrying," Gerald said, as she made for the bathroom to cleanse herself. "I'll go and telephone the school and tell them you have been unavoidably detained for half an hour. I'm sure they'll look after her until we get there. I'm coming with you, by the way. It's Belmont House isn't it?"

"Yes, yes," Nancy replied.

Before they left, Gerald asked her for one of her shoes. "Sorry, darling, but this afternoon is going to cost you a pair of shoes," he said as he proceeded to wrench the heel of the shoe loose by jamming it in the kitchen door. "That's your alibi," he said as they lowered themselves into his MG and drove off towards Belmont House.

Elizabeth was duly collected at 5.35 p.m., and introduced to Gerald as "the nice man who had rescued mommy from the terrible weather". They were soon all back at the farm. Harry Evans had just come back into the kitchen from his day's toil and was busily washing and scrubbing the evidence of his labours from his hands and arms.

"Oh, Harry, it was so lucky Mr De Beau came along," Nancy started. "I caught my heel in a grating at the bottom of the High Street and it almost came off," she continued. "I struggled with one stockinged foot, all my shopping to carry, and suddenly that terrible storm came down. I was drenched, like a drowned rat, then Mr De Beau appeared. He's dried me out at his house and so kindly taken me to fetch Elizabeth, and brought us both home. My car is still down in the town. I really don't know what I would have done without him," she concluded.

"Good God, you are lucky," Harry replied. "Sit yourself down, Mr De Beau, least we can do is offer you a cup of tea. In fact I'm sure if you can stop for dinner you're very welcome. We'll fetch the car up in the morning. It'll not hurt down there for a night."

For the first time in four hours, Nancy's pulse stopped racing. She was in the clear – Harry had no reason to disbelieve their story. He'd seen the damaged shoe and his mind was far too full of farming matters to dwell for too long on trivial domestic incidents.

During the next few years Gerald's business ideas came to fruition. The three machines he had shown Nancy were rebuilt and refurbished with the help of a local garage mechanic and were eagerly snapped up, much as Gerald had confidently predicted. Within two years, as peace settled across post-war England, Gerald had rented a warehouse on the outskirts of Chesterton and was now employing three full time mechanics and two labourers to refurbish the old implements. He had soon shed his seed selling responsibilities to concentrate fully on both the purchase of old machinery and the sales of his finished products. His name spread far and wide – 'the scrap man' they called him, but few farmers ever bought a new machine without first checking with Gerald about the availability and price of a rebuilt one. His unique knowledge of the farmers' needs soon led to his appointment as an agent for several machinery and tractor manufacturers. He was now able to offer either new or rebuilt, and turnover rocketed. Gerald was flying again.

In the autumn of 1946, Nancy and Harry were quietly having breakfast. It was Saturday morning. Harry was always slightly more relaxed about his farm duties at the weekend. "Harry, I want to ask you something," she began. "I'll fully understand if you say no but I've been offered a job, 9.30 to 3.30. I bumped into Mr De Beau when I went to the County Farms shop for pony food and he was telling me how well his machinery business is going but he's out on the road all day apparently, and needs someone to look after the office. With my bank background I could cope with it easily. We both know I'm not much good at this farming thing and Elizabeth's growing up a bit now so I would like to try it, as long as you don't mind. At least I would be doing something useful."

"Nancy, dear, whatever it takes to make you happy. There's no harm in trying it and if it doesn't work out there'll be no harm done. I'm sure you won't neglect Elizabeth's needs so give it a go." Harry's reply came without the knowledge that practically every other resident of Ampleford enjoyed.

"I reckons Harry Evans is grateful fer the help he's gettin' from the scrap man," was a recent remark floated across the market bar on waves of raunchy laughter.

Nancy's life was now almost fulfilled. Her affair with Gerald and her newfound employment were making life at Crest Farm so much more tolerable. Whilst they still kept their Thursday afternoon trysts at the cottage, the rear office at the warehouse was also put to regular convenient use, and at least her physical yearnings were now satisfied. In addition, she had access to Harry's money, she had social status, and she had Elizabeth. Any notion she had ever entertained of leaving Harry was firmly shelved.

So there she was – a regular at St Mark's Church on Sunday mornings, down on her knees in prayer and meditation. The real Nancy was in bed in Gerald's cottage every Thursday. Nancy was a hypocrite.

CHAPTER THREE

It was a cool September morning as Mary emerged from her infant slumbers. She yawned, rubbed her eyes with the backs of her hands and gazed wide-eyed at the ceiling. She snuggled down into the deep feather mattress and pulled the eiderdown up around her neck – she was comfy.

Although she was as bright as a button, she hadn't yet learnt to tell the time. She could count up to twenty, her colouring books were neat and tidy and she could just about print her name. Her sharp little brain was constantly demanding the answers to a multitude of questions which she fired constantly at Aunty Jo, Daddy and Gramps, but she hadn't quite mastered the functions of the clock. She relied on her instincts to tell her what she should be doing at any given time, and on the sights and sounds that filled her eyes and ears.

She could hear Aunty Jo lighting the fire in the parlour grate downstairs. She could hear the rattle of teacups and the sound of the tap filling the kettle. She could hear the screeching and squawking of the hens as Gramps released them from their sheds to scuttle across the paddocks in joyous freedom from their overnight captivity. The bleating of the sheep, the soft lowing of the cattle, and the faint grumble of a tractor starting up, these were the sounds that came wafting through her bedroom window. She could smell sizzling bacon – it was nearly time to get up.

She slid quietly on to the rug beside her bed, reached underneath for the little rosebud chamber potty, lifted her flannel nightie and did a quick wee. She pushed the potty back under the bed across the oilcloth floor covering, and scrambled quickly back to the warmth of her blankets. She would steal a few extra minutes of cuddly waking up time with her dolly. After a little while, she heard the creaking gate that led from the paddocks into the cottage garden, then the clang of the grain buckets as Gramps returned from his morning duties with the hens. She jumped out of bed, pushed her auburn, tousled head underneath the curtain and peered through the lead latticed window. Gramps was coming down the garden path, a bucket on each arm. Mary waved her tiny hand vigorously and Gramps raised a bucketed hand in reply. Now it really was time to get up.

"Come on, sleepy head," was Aunty Jo's greeting, as Mary crept into the parlour sucking the thumb of one hand, whilst clinging to her beloved dolly with the other one. In no time at all she was standing naked in the brown kitchen sink which had been filled with warm, sudsy water. "We'll soon have you shining like a new pin, my girl," said Aunty Jo as she brandished the soft pink flannel. She continued, "Let's wash under those armsies. Now turn round, under yer legsies, down between yer toesies. Now fer yer neck, chin up, chin down. Let's have a look at them ears – for God's sake, our Mary, will you stand still?"

Mary was soon curled up by the parlour fire, wrapped tightly in a warm fleecy towel, sipping a mug of sweet, milky tea, and shining, as promised, like a new pin. "Mommy came to see me when I was asleep last night."

Aunty Jo swallowed hard, "Did she now? Well, that's lovely."

"She said I'll be going to school soon and I must be a good girl."

"Well, that's true, next week it is you know."

Mary half closed her eyes. "Last Christmas morning after Santa had been, Mommy said that by this time next year I'll have been at school for three months. Is that how long it is 'till Santa comes again?"

"That's exactly right, you clever thing," came the reply.

"If I'm a good girl at school will he bring me a big new Teddy to be friends with Dolly, 'cos I think she's a bit lonely sometimes?"

"I'm sure he will," said Aunty Jo.

"Do the angels ever let anyone go after they've gone to live with them 'cos Mommy was there, but she was gone when I woke up?"

"Not really, sweetheart. I've never known it anyway."

"Well, it's just not fair, I'll never go and live with them. You won't go and live with them will you, Aunty?"

"Course not, I'm here living with you and that'll do for a bit, thank you very much."

Aunty Jo was pleased that Mary had been dreaming about Joan. It indicated that she still had her mother in her mind's eye – she was not forgotten. She watched her fill her tummy with boiled egg and toasted soldiers, pull on her little overalls and wellingtons, and scamper into the orchard to play with the dogs. Aunty Jo was on duty today, so Mary would be dropped off at Molly Perkins' where she would stay and play with Billy until 2 o'clock. In that way Molly had been an absolute brick during the previous few months. She was always there to help. Aunty Jo wasn't entirely happy with the arrangement – she wished that Billy was more normal – but she had no alternative other than to tolerate things.

There was certainly no offer of assistance with Mary from the Evans' at the farm. Harry had once mentioned to

Nancy that "young Mary at the cottage seems a bit lonely at times". He was soon shot down in flames.

"I don't want Elizabeth mixing there. I can't see the point in paying fees at Belmont House to educate her with the daughters of the professional classes, for her to come home and play with some yokel farm labourer's daughter."

Harry backed off, happy to leave domestic matters to Nancy and get on with running the farm, but not before saying, "She's such a pretty little girl, all auburn curls and blue eyes, and they've suffered so much in recent months."

"Well, let's just keep things as they are," Nancy snapped. "They seem to me to be coping pretty well with that district nurse living there and, let's face it, they are work people, Harry. They do their job, you look after them with wages and housing and so on, but it doesn't mean we have to mix with them. One day, when that Mary's scrubbing floors, our Elizabeth will be one of the wealthiest landowners in the county. They belong in different worlds, Harry, and it isn't fair to either of them to mix them up."

At that she flounced out of the room. It irked Nancy to hear Harry describe Mary as pretty with auburn curls and blue eyes, although it was the truth. In comparison Elizabeth was quite plain, having inherited Harry's angular features, sallow complexion, and straight dark hair. She was not a bit like her mother except in her mannerisms and her 'la-de-dah' turns of phrase. Her world was already dominated by an obsession with her pony. She had joined the local pony club and her conversations were littered with the Fionas, Charlottes and Harriets she met there. Nancy revelled in the social intercourse that being a parent at Belmont House brought with it. By now she was deeply involved in her affair with Gerald but it had not come without cost.

As the months had rolled by, the entire population of Ampleford had become aware of the circumstances of Nancy's relationship with Gerald de Beau. As well as the fact that she now had less time on her hands for church meetings, coffee mornings and charity committees, she was also far less welcome. The dowager ladies of the village, the matriarchs at the upper echelons of Ampleford society, did not approve. She found herself cruelly voted off the committees and would often learn of little soirees and 'at homes' to which she had not been invited. To some extent her involvement as a parent at Belmont House, where the social scene was less parochial, had compensated, but when she and Harry were excluded from the guest list of the wedding of the daughter of Major Harcourt, a close neighbour and landowner, she was mortified. Nancy was not daft – she knew the reason perfectly well but could hardly discuss it with Harry. The fact was, she had made her own bed and would now have to get on with lying on it. Post-war rural England was not 'avant garde'. The unwritten rules were there and as hypocritical as most of Nancy's antagonists were, they were also savagely unforgiving. Nancy's affair was the talk of the county.

Mary's childhood was becoming inextricably entwined with that of Billy Perkins. It was worrying enough that she spent so much of her infant time at Molly's farm, playing with Billy. It was even more worrying for Aunty Jo when she found out that Mary and Billy were to be in the same class at school. Although Billy had been at school for two years, at the end of his first year he had been kept down to spend a further year in the first group and now, at the end of his second year, he was to be kept down again – a seven-year-old with the five-year-olds. Aunty Jo had sensed Billy's tendency to cling to Mary, to willingly take instructions from her, to let her dictate the course of their playtimes together and to pathetically follow her, sheep-like, around the yard and barns at Molly's patch. One factor stopped Aunty Jo from taking steps to separate Mary and Billy – Mary simply didn't mind. She never once complained that Billy was a nuisance or a burden to her and she never once displayed any reluctance to be in his company. In fact, quite the reverse. At every opportunity she would show concern for his welfare, tying his boot laces, wiping his nose, and once bathing his scratched knees when he had fallen over while Molly was busy in the fields.

Aunty Jo reasoned that there was no point in preaching care, compassion and kindliness to Mary on the one hand, and then parting her from the one person on whom she could lavish those gifts. In her innocent, tender, unsullied mind, Mary saw nothing strange about Billy and, given the lovely, caring nature she had inherited from her mother, she found nothing irritating in his company. Billy, for his part, simply loved her. She never scolded or screeched at him, she didn't lose her patience or her temper with him, and she didn't make unachievable demands of him. She would hold his hand and help him across the brook. She was the kindest human being he was ever in contact with, and he gladly obeyed her and followed her everywhere. The closest Mary ever came to criticising Billy would be a remark such as: "He's bloomin' hopeless, Aunty Jo. He can't tie his boots yet and his mom's still wiping his bottom, and he's *seven*! I don't know what he would do without his mom and me." The word 'me' screamed out at Aunty Jo but, instinctively, she knew that Mary's involvement with Billy was completely natural and wholesome. Here was a bright, sparkly, good-natured little girl of five, mature way beyond her years, taking care of a less fortunate little boy of seven who had the mental capacity of a three-year-old.

Furthermore, she did not complain about it. For the moment Aunty Jo saw no reason to interfere.

Ampleford School was a typical Victorian built, red brick village school, examples of which can be seen in a thousand villages and towns across England. It was designed to accommodate one hundred children from five to eleven years old, although quite a few who didn't switch to Chesterton High or the Secondary Modern school at eleven stayed on to complete their education, leaving Ampleford at fifteen. Mary took to school like a duck takes to water – she relished every minute of it. Raring to go every morning, she would urge Aunty Jo to hurry up. "We've got to pick Billy up, you know."

"Good God, girl, it only takes fifteen minutes and it's only ten past eight. You'll be there before they've unlocked the gates one of these mornings. I can see it coming off."

Mary's teacher, Mrs Slater, thought she was delightful, "such a sensible little girl and so interested in everything we do". She would not admit it but it would be fair to say that Mary's presence had cut her workload with Billy Perkins by at least fifty per cent. He was now making plasticine models and working with raffia, and any wavering of concentration would attract a scowl from Mary that controlled him like nothing else. It was a good job that Billy spent a lot of time with Mr Biggs, the school gardener – at least it gave Mary a few brief times when she need only concern herself with her own activities.

Billy was an absolute star in the school garden, and Mr Biggs welcomed him warmly and pulled him in as often as possible. Give him a hoe, a rake or a spade and he was like a programmed automaton. He would slog non-stop for two or three hours, sweat dripping from his nose, cultivating huge areas of ground that would normally have taken a boy of his age two or three days. One of the teachers had once cruelly remarked, "Billy Perkins is a square peg in a square hole where the garden is concerned, after all isn't that where scarecrows are supposed to be". One look at Billy and you knew exactly what he meant. Everything about Billy was slightly larger than it should have been. His head, topped with masses of unruly red hair, appeared slightly too big for his body and it seemed to wobble as he moved. His tongue was slightly too big for his mouth causing a slow but constant dribble over a slightly too large lower lip. The dribble was contained by a relentless periodic wipe with the cuff of his right sleeve. His arms were slightly too long to be normal, carrying hands that were simply huge, and his feet were of similar proportion on the end of slightly bowed legs. He rarely had a full set of buttons on either his shirt or his trousers, the latter often sporting large, unmatching patches. His footwear, winter and summer, was ankle-high black boots, and within an hour of putting them on, his socks would have gone to sleep, and there they would stay for the rest of the day. Nevertheless, as the year of 1947 rolled away, Billy was making a little progress with some of his school work. He was immensely proud of the bowls of hyacinths he had planted under the supervision of Mr Biggs. He had tended them carefully in the school greenhouse, and grinned with uncontained satisfaction as he distributed them around the classrooms in December. He didn't have to say a word – his swagger spoke volumes. "How 'bout that then, p'raps I ent se useless arter all."

There were the occasional lapses. The school morning ended at 11.45 when the infants would troop into the dining room for their school dinner. The school split into three and went in at forty-five minute intervals, with the little ones going first. At 12.30 p.m., weather permitting, there would be practically a full hour of playtime, and at 1.30 they would all be sat on their bottoms in the hall whilst Mrs

Slater read them a story for about fifteen minutes. At this point, out would come the little canvas beds and they were all expected to go to sleep for about half an hour or so. Absolute quiet was demanded by Mrs Slater at this time, total silence. She was a stern yet kind lady, well into middle age, with tightly permed hair and large spectacles. She was an old-fashioned disciplinarian and the slightest noise would send her volcanic. The offender would be yanked by their ear and made to stand outside the door.

Billy had eaten a big breakfast that morning, a huge bowl of porridge, which he had devoured like a savage gannet. School dinner was minced beef and onions with mashed swede, followed by stewed prunes and custard. Billy filled his little belly for the second time in six hours until it was taut. He should have put up his hand when the little canvas beds were being brought out – he didn't. He ignored the sharp little pain in his lower abdomen and the shifting of gut contents as the pain went away. He lay down on the little bed and went to sleep. When he woke up twenty minutes later, the dreadful realisation of what had happened was immediate. The warm, liquid sensation in his trousers was real, he wasn't dreaming.

"Mair," he whispered, but there was no response from Mary who was lying on the little bed beside him, covered by a grey blanket, with only her auburn topped head visible. "Mair," he pleaded a little louder.

Her eyes slowly opened as her tiny index finger came up to her pursed lips, "Shhhh." Her advice was ignored.

"Mair, I'se shit meself," Billy uttered. "I'se jus' woke up and I'se shit meself."

"You'll have to tell Mrs Slater," Mary urged.

At this, the volcano erupted. "Who's talking in the corner over there? Come on, stand up, who's talking?" Billy leapt to his feet and stood by his bed. "Right, Billy Perkins,

I'll soon deal with you," she spat, and went marching purposefully across the hall. Before she had reached halfway she hit a brick wall of stench, stopping her dead in her tracks. By now an offending steaming brown dollop, the size of a tea plate, had dropped from Billy's trousers on to the wooden block floor. Horror and disgust spread across her face. "Get out, get out," bawled Mrs Slater. "Go and stand by the front gate and stay there until your mother comes. Everybody stay exactly where you are, I'm going to fetch Mr Biggs." She struggled to contain the retching urges of her stomach, and gratefully sucked in the fresh air as she strode across the school yard in the direction of the school garden, where she would find Mr Biggs. Mr Biggs doubled as caretaker as well as gardener, and he soon appeared with a bucket of sand and a shovel. Later he would return with a mop and bucket filled with hot water and Dettol. Evidence of Billy's misfortune was soon removed, all the hall windows were opened and, with the exception of the faint smell of disinfectant which lingered for days, everything was soon as before. It was 2.45 p.m. and Billy stood in his own filth at the school gate, head hung pitifully in abject shame.

It would be 3.30 p.m. before Molly came to pick them up, and it was starting to rain. By now Mrs Slater had led her class back to the crisper, cleaner air of their own classroom where she read to them again, and they would sing a little song. After a few minutes she noticed Mary Jones with her right hand reaching earnestly into the air. "What is it, Mary? What's the matter?" she asked.

"Please, Mrs Slater, can I take Billy his coat 'cos its raining and he'll get wet."

"Yes, child, yes, hurry up, and tell him to stand just inside the front door if you like." She found herself turning away from the class as she swallowed, and a tear welled up in her eye. Such tender compassion from one so young had hit a nerve with Mrs Slater. She could not think of another single human being, herself included, who would want to go within a hundred yards of Billy Perkins in his present state. "That girl must have been touched by the Angel Gabriel himself," she murmured to herself as she brought her emotions under control, wiped her eye and continued with her duties.

The months and years rolled by. Billy's and Mary's childhoods continued to unfold along a path of mutual concern for each other's welfare, even though the concern was heavily one-sided. Aunty Jo remained ever watchful but any concerns she might have harboured were always soothed by a succession of glowing reports from Mary's school teachers. Furthermore, her mature, common sense behaviour around the cottage was a constant joy.

An incident in the summer of 1947 did set alarm bells ringing for a little while. Billy was proudly showing Mary a clutch of tiny bantam chicks that had been hatched the day before in the barn. He pushed his hands down between the bales of straw where the little bantam hen had made her nest and hatched her little family. She pecked and scratched viciously in protection of her brood, but Billy's fist emerged triumphantly with one of the miniscule chicks. "Put yer hand out, Mair, hold it."

Mary stretched the palm of her hand out and Billy placed the bewildered, fluffy little bird on to it. It was weightless with huge eyes and little claws that scratched the surface of her skin. Mary was enthralled at the wonder of this tiny little bird but was soon pleading with Billy to put it back with its mom. "Would yer like to see me snake now, Mair?" he enquired.

"You haven't got a snake, Billy. You're telling lies, you know you are."

"I 'ave, I 'ave, I tell you, I'se got a snake, Mair, honest I 'as if you wants to see it."

Mary thought she was on safe ground when she said, "Come on then, but I don't believe you." At this, Billy promptly undid his trouser buttons and proudly produced his willy from his pants. Like everything else about Billy, it was slightly too large.

"Put it away, Billy, it's horrible," Mary said with tones of disgust in her voice.

"'As you got a snake, Mair?" Billy enquired.

"No, I haven't and I don't want one thank you. Now just put it away will you?" By now she was shouting at him in horror. She turned to leave but as she moved towards the barn door it opened. There stood Molly, attracted by the commotion. "Billy's got his snake out," Mary blurted. "It's horrible."

"Snake, is it?" Molly snapped. "Snake, eh, we'll soon see about that." Her face went crimson with rage, as realising what had happened, she yanked hold of Billy by a tuft of his red hair. Bang – she thwacked him across the ear with her free hand. "Take that to start with, you dirty little beast you, snake is it? We'll soon see about that." She continued to smack him all the way across the yard to the washhouse where she picked up the dolly stick. "To bed, my lad," she screeched, as she belted his legs with the stick. "Don't you move 'till tomorrow morning or I'll kill you stone dead, I will."

Aunty Jo worried herself silly for several days. "Where's Billy then?" she had inquired when she collected Mary. Molly proceeded to regale the entire story. Mary sensed Aunty Jo's disquiet on the short journey up the hill to home, having witnessed her looks of horror as Molly had explained the reason for Billy being shut in his bedroom.

"I've seen Billy's willy before, Aunty," she blurted, "when he poohed his pants at school. His mom stood him on the back yard, over the drain, took all his clothes off and put the hosepipe on him and I saw it then. It's sort of funny and horrible – I'll never let him show it me again." Nevertheless, Aunty Jo felt a word with Dr Powell would be appropriate.

"It's perfectly understandable for you to worry about it, Nurse Jones," he said, "but I would urge you not to get things out of perspective. If I had a pound for every time an eight-year-old boy has shown his willy to the little girl next door, believe me, I would be a millionaire several times over."

Aunty Jo's anxieties were relieved but she vowed to keep a close eye on things. She need not have bothered. The incident was the first and last time that anything remotely sexual occurred between Mary and Billy in their entire lives – lives that were destined to be closely entwined for evermore.

Nineteen fifty-two brought a parting of the ways for Billy and Mary, as far as school was concerned. Mary had passed her eleven plus examination and was off to Chesterton High School in September. Everyone at home and all her teachers at school were so proud of her. At eleven years old she was such a wholesome, well-balanced girl, easily able to switch from her school gymslip and her homework, into her dungarees, to help with the poultry and general work around the farm. Although the minimum school leaving age was fifteen, Billy was given special dispensation to leave Ampleford at fourteen to help his mother on the farm. A letter from Mr Wood, the headmaster, did the trick. It contained one all-embracing sentence, 'This boy will never read or write as long as he lives, he simply has not got the mental capacity'.

An incident at the school in the June of that year was the motivating force that prompted the headmaster to write the letter. Ampleford School had three play yards; one at the front of the school where the five and six year olds played happily together, and two at the rear of the school where the boys played on the one side and the girls played on the other. These backyards were separated by a four foot brick wall. The thinking was that, as they got older, boys were so much rougher than girls and therefore should be segregated. To some extent it was true. Billy had been an object of ridicule from a very early age. His red hair, his size, his unfortunate stupidity, his shabby clothes, and his lack of a father, all set him apart from the rest of the children. Ampleford, like all schools, had its element of bullying ringleaders and when they had tired of their games of football, or Cowboys and Indians, Billy was an easy source of amusement. More often than not, Billy didn't know he was being ragged. He would gleefully join in his own humiliation, laughing heartily as his schoolmates lampooned and scoffed around him.

"Billy Perkins got no dad, got no dad, Billy Perkins got no dad, nah-nah-nah-nah-nah," they would all chant as they danced around him, pushing him from one side of the circle to the other. Billy would act limp, like a rag doll, offering no resistance to their shoving. "Billy can't read, Billy can't write, Billy wets the bed in the middle of the night," was another verse that was often cruelly employed. Billy just joined in. He thought it was huge fun – Mary did not.

Mary's and Billy's days at Ampleford would soon be coming to an end but at lunchtime on that June day, she heard the 'Billy Perkins got no dad' chant coming from the other side of the playground. She scrambled to the top of the dividing wall, her tousled, auburn hair a fitting symbol to her rage.

"Stop it, leave him alone, just leave him alone or I'll get a teacher," she squealed. If anything, the pace and volume of the chant quickened as Billy was heaved violently round the inside of the circle, like a dead sheep. "Stop it, stop it, you nasty lot," she shrieked, and then "For God's sake Billy, stand up for yourself, stop them, Billy, sock them one or something, just stop them."

As always, Billy did exactly what Mary told him – with devastating effect. The next time he went stumbling across their frenzied circle, the 'dead sheep' swung a huge right hand punch into the mouth of the boy who was in the process of pushing him back in the opposite direction. A repeat performance on the other side of the circle meant that two of them were now rolling across the schoolyard, bellowing in agony. The sight of one boy spitting teeth and blood on to the yard, and the other, face ashen with the searing pain from a dislocated jaw, brought an instant veil of silence to the whole proceedings. A teacher appeared and both boys were quickly taken to hospital. Mary, still leaning over the wall, was in a state of shock at Billy's display of awesome physical power. She pleaded with the teacher, "It wasn't Billy's fault, sir, they wouldn't leave him alone. Please let me tell you what happened, it wasn't Billy's fault."

Early in the afternoon Mary was summoned to see Mr Wood, the headmaster. "Tell me exactly what happened, Mary," he said. As soon as Mary repeated the 'Billy's got no dad' chant, Mr Wood's demeanour softened. He believed everything that Mary had told him and no action was taken against Billy except a warning to keep his fists to himself in future. Mr Wood was already of a mind to arrange for Billy's early departure from school. The incident convinced him that Billy's continued presence at Ampleford School would serve no useful purpose. Billy would get bigger and stronger; he needed to be engaged in physical work as an outlet for his vigour. His school days were numbered.

Mary's seven weeks of summer holiday, before going to Chesterton High School, were idyllic – golden days which she was to remember for the rest of her life, in essence the last few weeks of her childhood.

Apart from a lovely day spent at the County Show with her dad, she spent the entire holiday helping with the harvest and giving Aunty Jo extra help around the cottage. She particularly enjoyed being with the men in the cornfields. They teased her a little, but generally spoiled her to bits. The binder was pulled round and round the field by a tractor, its sails rotating, gently turning the ripened corn on to the mower blades, and then sucking the severed crop up into a drum. There it was neatly tied in sheaves and then deposited back on to the field. Mary would help to pick up the sheaves and build four of them into a succession of wigwams around the field. They would then be left for a day or two for the sun to dry them. During these weeks the sun seemed to blaze continuously from a cloudless blue sky. This was a time that Mary wished could last forever, she was so happy, but of course, nothing lasts forever. Life moves on and so did Mary.

CHAPTER FOUR

Mary fitted in at Chesterton High as easily as she had at Ampleford seven years earlier. The mornings were a bit rushed because Aunty Jo needed to drop her in Ampleford by 8.15 a.m., so that she could catch the school bus. With Molly no longer sharing the duties of return transport, Aunty Jo had to collect her at 5 o'clock every afternoon. Dr Powell was only too happy to let her adjust her duties to accommodate these arrangements and also, when Aunty Jo was delayed, to allow Mary to wait at the surgery, just a short walk from the bus stop.

On the way home up the hill, Billy would often wave furiously as they drove past – still in the old Morris Minor. Regularly Aunty Jo would stop. "Want to come up to tea, Billy?" she would ask. "Go and tell your mom and I'll bring you back down in an hour or so."

Billy fled across the yard to tell his mom, his hair a red blur as he did his greyhound impersonation. He loved to go up to Mary's to tea and to tell them what he had been doing on the farm. He was always invited up to birthday parties and would stuff himself with fish paste sandwiches and jelly, then sit with a huge grin on his face, smothered with chocolate éclair or doughnut cream, just happy to be with friends, kids his own age and, particularly, to be close to Mary. On summer evenings he would often walk the half mile or so across the fields to Crest Farm Cottage. He would help Mary and Gramps with the chickens, have a glass of lemonade and skip back down home as soon as darkness loomed. Thus, Mary and Billy never lost contact and, as in their early childhood, Aunty Jo never once heard Mary complain that he was a nuisance. She had long since shed any anxieties she had nursed about the relationship and continued to take Billy to town, when necessary, to shop for his shirts, trousers, boots and socks, a job Molly had been only too pleased to be relieved of several years earlier.

"Jus' tell me what you'se spended and get 'im what you thinks," she would say. "We shall allus be internally grateful to you and Mary, Nurse, for the help you gis our Billy. One day there'll be a reckonin', jus' you rest insured about that."

As the school terms and the years rolled by, Mary had accepted her academic limitations. At Ampleford she had been a top dog, in the nicest possible way. At Chesterton her classmates included boys and girls destined to become doctors, dentists, lawyers and lecturers, heights that Mary would not achieve. Her favourite subjects were Biology, Maths and English Literature. Biology related easily to the farm animals and the wildlife and flowers she had grown up with. Maths she was comfortable with as she had a sharp, numerate brain, honed by the constant counting of eggs into sixes and twelves, thirty on a tray and twelve trays in a crate, sums she had been doing almost from babyhood. English Literature revealed her soul, helped by a marvellous teacher – her favourite – Mr Dobson. He had that rare, colourful gift of being able to bring his subject to life. His pupils would sit, transfixed, as he illuminated his lessons to a level that gripped their imaginations and within a few minutes of his lecture commencing, you could have heard a pin drop. Eventually he introduced Mary's class to

Shakespeare. A passage from King Richard II moved her almost to tears. It included the lines:

'This royal throne of kings, this sceptred isle,
This other Eden, demi-paradise,
This precious stone set in the silver sea,
This blessed plot, this earth, this realm, this England.'

Mary would close her eyes and could transport herself to the very highest point of Crest Farm on a summer's morning – sceptred isle, demi-paradise, precious stone, blessed plot – she knew exactly what William Shakespeare had meant. Earlier in the year she had discovered lines in A. E. Housman's 'A Shropshire Lad':

'What are those blue, remembered hills,
What spires, what farms are those?
That is the land of lost content,
I see it shining plain,
The happy highways where I went,
And cannot come again.'

Mary's flesh went goosey. She was amazed, aghast with wonder that these poets, remote, both dead, could so easily encapsulate the land on which she had been born and raised.

Furthermore, they so completely embraced her own feelings, and her own love for it. She lived on those blue, remembered hills, that demi-paradise. A mere fifteen years old she may have been, but Mary's roots were reaching down, reaching down to anchor her securely for life in Ampleford, on the fells and meadows of Crest Hill.

Mary's last two years at Chesterton High were two of the most fulfilling of her life so far. She sang in the choir, she played netball for the school team, she was fun to be with and popular with her fellow pupils – the principal reasons for her election as House Captain in her final year.

Whilst Mary was able to continue with her first love, Biology, and English Literature, her main work during those final years was in the Secretarial Department. She learnt to type and how to write shorthand. She learnt office skills and how to apply her Maths to commercial situations. She comfortably gained a highly commendable General Certificate of Education, and throughout those busy months she continued to help Gramps with the chickens, Aunty Jo with the housework, and kept closely in touch with Billy, forever mindful of his welfare.

Mary's passage through childhood and early adolescence brought virtually no contact at all with Elizabeth Evans at the farm, although one summer afternoon there was a notable exception. Elizabeth's passion for her horses was now deeply established. She had three horses and spent every spare waking moment tending them. One afternoon, during the school holiday period, Elizabeth was cantering around the orchard on a new young horse only recently broken in. Something spooked the fresh, young horse – it may have been a rabbit or a cat – and it started to prance and rear, throwing Elizabeth to the ground. She lay there, motionless. Mary had witnessed the incident from the cottage garden. She watched the horse charge off, jump the hedge from the orchard into the adjoining field, and gallop away out of sight. Mary immediately ran to Elizabeth's aid, just as she was regaining consciousness – she was winded, bruised and slightly concussed. Mary helped her into the cottage, sat her down and gave her a glass of water to sip.

"You are lucky," Mary said, "you might have broken your neck."

"Ring Mummy at the farm," Elizabeth replied. Nancy Evans was there in a matter of seconds and she quickly shepherded Elizabeth down the drive and back to the farm. Later in the day, her bumps suitably soothed, Elizabeth said, "Mary Jones was very kind, Mummy."

"Please don't tell me about it," Nancy replied. "I can't believe you've been inside that cottage. I just hope you haven't caught head lice or something, darling, that's all."

Shortly after this incident, Nancy and Harry separated. Nancy's affair with Gerald de Beau was now seven years old and Harry had long since come to terms with what had been happening. In the beginning he kept quiet counsel in the hope that it might all blow over, but it soon became patently obvious that this simply wasn't going to happen. It took him the best part of two years to admit to himself that things were drastically wrong. The signs were all there – her sudden total lack of interest in any physical intercourse with him for one.

Nevertheless it was several more months before he fully acknowledged that she was betraying him. He spoke to no-one about the matter during those empty, gnawing days, when the dreadful realisation of her philandering crystallized in his mind. Eventually he plucked up the courage to go and quietly discuss his fears with his solicitor, Mr William Smythe-Roberts. He was an old and trusted friend as well as being the family solicitor. By this time, Nancy's affair was some three years down the road.

"Harry, my dear friend," he began, "I am deeply saddened by what you have told me, however, it would be dishonest of me to pretend that I had no inkling of this matter. I would not be so disingenuous with such an old and respected client. I fully understand and admire your reasons for wanting to keep your marriage intact – Elizabeth would be the main casualty of a separation. My advice would be, if you can endure the pain, for you to continue on your present course, do nothing, say nothing, and hope that eventually this thing will burn itself out. They often do."

Harry shrugged his shoulders. "I just needed to talk to someone, Bill, really. I've no intention of taking any action about it at the moment, but it can't go on for ever."

It did go on – for another four years. Nancy and Gerald often talked about her moving in with him but they always came up against an obstacle called Elizabeth. There was no question of Elizabeth moving away from Crest Farm and her beloved horses, but Gerald and Nancy comforted each other in the knowledge that she was growing up. One day she would be mature enough to cope. They did not anticipate that in the spring of 1951, soon after Elizabeth's twelfth birthday, she was going to have to learn to cope.

Harry Evans had gone to market on the Tuesday of that April week. Just before returning home, needing to relieve his bladder, he visited the market toilets. As it was jammed with a jostling throng of farmers on exactly the same mission, Harry had to wait a few moments, with several others, for a place at the gulley. Amidst the din of conversation he heard a voice from the far end, "I feels a bit sorry for him now. Christ, he must know they'm shagging their arses off at every opportunity they gets. If he don't know now, he's dafter than I ever thought he was."

There was a discreet cough or two as some of the farmers realised what the conversation was about, and who had just walked in to join them. Within a few brief seconds the lavatory was gripped by a deathly silence. The source of the remark, a middle-aged sheep farmer, quickly buttoned his fly, pulled his cap down firmly on his head, and slunk, head bowed, through the door.

Enough was enough, Harry's humiliation was complete. He knew, as did everyone else, who they were talking about. That evening he asked Nancy to leave as soon as possible. "I can't see the point in carrying on with the deceit and the lies," he said. "For God's sake, we are grown up people, why pretend any longer. I've ignored what's been going on for long enough and there comes a time when one has to hang the consequences and just clear the air. Your being here isn't relevant any more – there's no love, no respect, no future. I don't think the last fifteen years have meant a shred to you, Nancy. I am assuming you will agree that Elizabeth should remain here, her family home, her birthright, and of course with the horses which she loves. You will have complete access to her, of course, and I will discuss financial arrangements with Bill Smythe-Roberts tomorrow. Quite simply, Nancy, I want you off Crest Farm tomorrow – tonight if possible."

Nancy's reply was instantaneous and without a shred of emotion. "I'll be out in an hour and will fetch my things tomorrow. I should never have come here in the first place." Quiet, deliberate words, with that final phrase that was so devastatingly true.

Elizabeth coped easily with her mother's departure. She had known for quite some time that Gerald was a special friend, and had long since become used to calling him 'Uncle Gerald'. She visited them regularly at the cottage by the river and often stayed over for the night. Crest Farm remained her home, however, and as she rode across its broad acres she began to develop a sense of pride in the possession of it. Even at fourteen and fifteen years old she began to think, in her quieter moments, that one day all this would be hers.

Nancy's divorce settlement included a walloping lump sum – somewhere around £20,000 was agreed upon. Harry could afford it. Also the monthly income of £200 was well within his compass, but what worried him more than anything, though, was Nancy's insistence that in return for her not pursuing any claim on the farm land, house, or business, he must sign it all over to Elizabeth's ownership on her twenty-first birthday. In spite of his misgivings he had little option. Gerald de Beau had secured the services of an eminent lawyer to act for Nancy, and Harry quickly realised that if she so desired, she could spark the sale of the whole caboodle, lock, stock and barrel. He took some comfort from the fact that half of everything belonged to George, his brother, but spent many sleepless nights worrying himself silly as to what would happen to George's wealth as both brothers had once made wills leaving their respective shares to each other. Marrying Nancy had blown that arrangement sky high although, whilst Harry had changed his will to Nancy's benefit, George assured him that his remained as before. Harry now worried that if George died before Elizabeth was twenty-one, leaving him in the ownership of the entire farm, he would then have to sign everything over to his daughter – personally, he would be penniless.

His worst fears were realised. George did die quietly in 1960, aged seventy-two. What started as a heavy cold, quickly progressed to influenza, bronchitis and pneumonia. His lungs collapsed, and George passed away in Chesterton General Hospital in December of that year. George had never been a particularly robust type of man, his life devoted entirely to the farm and the church. Although he had disliked his sister-in-law intensely, he was far too much of a gentleman to show it. When she had left eight years previously, he felt quiet relief, his only remarks to his brother being, "More's the pity you ever met her and brought her here in the first place. You'll have a deal of tidying up to do now, that's for certain."

George's will revealed exactly what he had promised – his entire estate went to his brother. Harry now owned the entire farm, but for how long? Under the terms of his divorce settlement he must turn his title to Crest Farm over to his daughter and she would be twenty-one in a few short months. Harry was sixty-three years old, and he accepted that at some time in the future Elizabeth would have been his heir, but at twenty-one he did not see her as a safe pair of hands – in fact, precisely the opposite. Elizabeth was headstrong and selfish, and furthermore she possessed most of her mother's flighty ways. Harry was decidedly uneasy about her associations, and her obsession with horses had escalated, an obsession for which Harry was required to keep footing the bill. Three point-to-pointers and two novice steeplechasers were now part of the growing stable at Crest Farm. It had to be said, however, that Elizabeth was totally dedicated to their welfare, riding out at half past five every morning, mucking out, feeding and grooming, all tasks she gladly shared with the girl groom who was employed as part of the farm staff. Moderate successes, the odd winner and several seconds and thirds served only to fuel Elizabeth's mania for the racing scene, and her infatuation for the people within it.

Harry Evans had indulged Elizabeth's every whim where the horses were concerned. After Nancy's departure he was, understandably, keen to retain his daughter's affection, and each and every request for new horses, stable blocks, horse boxes and equipment, was usually quickly met. Now, with Elizabeth's premature inheritance imminent, the alarm bells began to clang. The horses contributed nothing to the income of Crest Farm, in fact, quite the opposite – they were a substantial financial drain on the business, and Elizabeth knew nothing of day-to-day farm management. Her head was crammed only with pedigrees, form, fitness, handicaps, the going, and all the paraphernalia of horse racing. Harry also saw the hangers-on, the racing riff-raff, oily characters in shabby clothes, driving beat up motor cars: the racing 'hoi polloi', unable by a million miles to afford the finance required for any direct involvement with the sport. They hovered and hung like moths round a candle, latching on to the slipstream of any set up with a sniff of money about it. The freebies – drink, food, transport to the races – and the illusion that they were on the inside, all served as irresistible attractions.

One such character, Michael Mason, twenty-five years old, concerned Harry greatly. His family were shady to say the least, livestock dealers of dubious reputation. They occupied a rented farm at Calverton, some eight miles away. Michael's father would buy and sell anything to earn a shilling. His land was too poor to grow anything or feed stock profitably, and so for years he had scoured the livestock markets within a fifty mile radius, on a daily basis, looking for bargains. He would buy cattle in ones and twos from here, there and everywhere, and then match them into larger bunches to be sold at the big store cattle sales held every month at Ampleford. To be profitable it needed skills that were verging on the very edge of sharp practice. Michael's father, Mike senior, was a man the Evans brothers had always shunned, 'not to be trusted', 'couldn't lie straight in bed', were some of the aspersions hung round his neck.

In his teens, young Michael had been quite a useful jockey, his services much sought after by some of the gentlemen owners of point-to-pointers. His own family simply did not have the financial clout to buy and race horses, and once Michael matured and his weight began to rocket, he was left stranded. On one hand, he had been deeply bitten by the horse bug and the thrills of racing – the addictive surge of adrenalin through his veins as a horse he supported came over the last fence in front. On the other hand, he had insufficient money to pursue that addiction and had latched on to the situation at Crest Farm some two years before.

He readily offered his services to drive the box, ride out in the mornings, and generally perform the tasks associated with the title 'Head Lad'. In addition, Elizabeth found him quite attractive. Elizabeth was not exactly overwhelmed by suitors. She was handsome rather than pretty, with a boyish sort of face and a slim figure that was not unattractive, but unfortunately there was an edge to her nature that most boys found repelling: the disdain for anyone less well off that verged on scorn, the air of superiority that gave her the confidence to tongue-lash anyone who displeased her, and her childish petulance when things did not always go her way. She was not a good loser, and in the sport of horse racing she had ample opportunities to display that flaw in her character.

In the summer of 1957, Michael Mason had only recently come on to the scene at Crest Farm. Mary was a year away from leaving school and at the weekends she still helped with the poultry. Gramps was now nearly eighty and, although he was hale and hearty, his advancing age meant that one of the farm hands now had to give regular daily assistance with the birds. On Saturdays Mary had taken on the task of running a market stall for the Evans brothers, selling their surplus eggs. She had been encouraged by Molly Perkins who ran the vegetable stall. On Sundays, Gramps and Mary managed the poultry feeding and the egg collecting on their own. One summer Sunday afternoon Mary found the grain bins in the paddocks empty so she would have to fetch wheat in buckets from the granary above the barn. She walked the short distance through the orchard to the rear of the barn, and quietly climbed the sandstone steps to the granary above. As she unlatched the door, she heard the noise of a lorry driving into the farmyard and pulling up in front of the barn. She began to fill her buckets from the sacks of wheat and then suddenly realised that someone had entered the barn area below and closed the big timber door behind them. She heard a voice – Elizabeth's. "We must be quick, no time for any fancy stuff. Dad could be out here at any time."

Mary froze – should she creep out and risk being discovered or should she stay and lie low? She chose the latter. Below her feet were timber floorboards, a hundred years old. As she sat on a half empty sack of wheat, she could see the barn below through a two inch gap in those ancient boards. She was transfixed – Michael Mason and Elizabeth were lying between the hay bales. Elizabeth's blouse was unbuttoned, her brassiere unhooked, her breasts fully exposed. Michael had his hand down the front of her unbuttoned jodphurs, his fingers visibly active, and Elizabeth's hand was similarly engaged in Michael's crotch. The episode of mutual masturbation lasted for less than ten minutes when, their lusts satisfied, their passions quenched, they left the barn.

Mary was mortified – she wished she hadn't been there. Her senses were filled with feelings of disgust and guilt. She hadn't lived her entire life on a farm and not learnt the facts of life, and had long since switched on to the fact that the human race often indulged in sex for pleasure. Procreation was more often than not the last thing in their minds – sex could be fun. Nevertheless, somehow, she felt that the episode she had just witnessed was somewhat tacky and unwholesome, performed with little affection, something she would like to wash away, something from which she would like to cleanse herself.

That evening Aunty Jo noticed Mary's quiet mood. "You look a bit pale tonight, our Mary," she said, "you feeling alright?"

"For God's sake, leave me alone," Mary screamed back at her and fled off up to her room.

"Well, God alive, what did I say to deserve that?" said Aunty Jo.

As Mary had eventually left the granary that afternoon with her buckets of grain, and made her way back through the orchard, she had been spotted by Elizabeth who was looking through the kitchen window. She saw the buckets and guessed their contents. A dreadful realisation slowly dawned upon her and ice cold anger snaked up her spine, the questions racing in quickening succession across her brain. Was she? Did she? Could she? Had she? The bitch, the spying little bitch! Elizabeth quickly realised her dilemma. She had no proof that Mary had spied, and couldn't be totally certain that she had. To chastise her would be to spill the beans anyway. She would have to live with it and wonder, and that made her furiously angry, with no-one to vent her anger upon. That anger never left her – it was still fresh and festering in her mind two and a half years later when she inherited the farm.

CHAPTER FIVE

Aunty Jo would never miss Sunday morning service at St Mark's if she could help it. Hers was a simple faith which she could never have explained. "It just seems like the right way to end one week and start the next, and I know I am all the stronger for it," she often said. Unlike his sister, Dick simply did not possess that faith. Certainly, he led a Christian life, a life filled with love and compassion for his family, his workmates and the animals in his care. His Christianity was, however, remote – he was not a devout churchgoer.

As a small child, Mary had often been to family services and attended Sunday School, and as she grew older, Aunty Jo encouraged her to go along on Sunday mornings. However, as her teenage years unfolded, her attendances waned. She could always find something more important – more interesting to do. Faced with following the examples set by the two most influential people in her young life, where the church was concerned Mary was with her dad.

The family often visited Joan's grave, set beneath the spreading oaks and close to the sandstone wall by the lych gate of St Mark's churchyard. Christmas and Mothers' Day were never missed, nor the anniversary of Joan's death. On her birthday and their wedding anniversary, Dick would go quietly down on his own.

As Mary grew older and more independent, she would occasionally slip into the churchyard alone with a little posy to place beneath the headstone. By now the memories of her mother had long since all but melted away. In the recesses of her mind she could imagine the vague shape of her mother's figure and the soft waves of her light brown hair, but the sound of her voice was no more, lost to Mary for all eternity. Her perception of her mother was now largely shaped by the photographs she had and by what her dad and Aunty Jo had told her. "There wasn't a nicer lady ever born than your mom," Aunty Jo had said, "not a shred of nastiness or envy in her body. If you turn out anywhere near like her, our Mary, you'll be alright."

By now, in her middle teenage years, Mary had reached the age of reason and rationality. "How can I try to be like someone I've never known?" she asked.

"You can't," came the reply from Aunty Jo. "You don't have to try to be nice, it comes natural, you either are or you aren't, and everyone shows their true colours at sometime. Don't get big-headed but me and your dad are really proud of you so far, so just keep being yourself. There's a great deal of your mom about you, that's a fact."

Mary loved her home, her family and her school friends, and she had a tremendous zest for life. In her quieter moments, however, she was often overcome by pangs of anxiety, by an empty, hollow seething in the tummy. "Why my mom? If she was so lovely, why her?" These moments did not last long and she would soon start to count her blessings. Nevertheless, she could not help asking the unanswerable. "If there is this great God, this God of love and understanding, if he has all these fantastic powers to fight evil, then where's my mom?" Mary did not dwell on these things – life was fun, far too enjoyable to brood, but as far as the church and religion were concerned, there were too many unanswered questions for her liking. Furthermore, she was old enough and sharp enough to have identified the churchgoing hypocrites, and she couldn't help thinking that the vicar seemed to visit the wealthy far more often than he visited the poor and deprived who needed him most.

Mary had now turned seventeen, and during the course of her Saturday morning market duties she had been noticed by Philip Manders. Philip was thirty-five years old, a shooting, fishing and rugby man, married with two daughters. He had a chameleon like talent which enabled him to adjust his manners to suit the company of the moment. He was at ease with both the landed gentry and the cattle drovers, and had a likeable charm. He was a partner in the firm of Barker and Bright, Estate Agents and Livestock Auctioneers, and was an auctioneer of some repute. He had served with great distinction during the latter years of the war as a captain in the Royal Fusiliers. Being from a farming family, he had brought to Barker and Bright not only the dash and verve of his youth, the organisation, experience and discipline of his Army training, but also his comfort and compatibility with country people, and country ways. He was hard but fair in all his business dealings, and was generally a popular member of Ampleford's rural scene.

Philip's eyes had lit upon Mary whilst browsing around the market one Saturday morning. There she was – all crisp white blouse and gleaming smile, shiny shoes and shiny hair. He had noticed how quick and nimble she was, her busy, efficient manner behind the counter of her stall and the ease with which she dealt with her customers, totting up their purchases, taking their money and giving them their change.

It was May 1958, and Mary was in the process of doing her 'O' Levels at school. Philip Manders, on Saturday shopping duty, stopped off at her stall. "It's Mary Jones from Crest Farm, isn't it?"

"Yes, that's me," she replied.

"Mary, I suspect you may be at school and involved in your exams at the moment, but I wondered whether you have a job or some career in mind, and if you are going to leave school in July. Please give it some thought, but I would be delighted to interview you for a position in the office at Barker and Bright. You would be very much involved in the livestock market side of the business and with your background I feel sure you would quickly fit into the scheme of things."

Mary looked at the man who had addressed her. She noticed his ruddy face, his reddish hair topped by his check cap, set at a slightly cheeky angle. He wore a check sports coat, together with a similar check shirt. His corduroy trousers, brown cavalry boots and moleskin waistcoat completed the very essence of a man from the agricultural world. Most importantly, she had quite liked what she saw. "Well," she replied to his question, "I have already spoken to the manager of two banks and a building society in the town. They have told me to go back when my 'O' Level results are through. I have already finished my typing and shorthand tests and they are quite good results, I think." She was being modest.

"Now listen," Philip Manders responded, "get your exams out of the way and then, if you think you might be interested, pop into the office and ask for me, Philip Manders, and we can chat about things in a bit more detail."

"Ok," came her reply, "I will do that."

"Good luck with those exams then, and I'll expect to see you sometime, perhaps, at the end of next month. Don't forget now," Philip Manders concluded and moved to walk away.

"Oh, Mr Manders," cried Mary, remembering her manners, "thank you very much for the opportunity, and I *will* come."

If truth were known, Mary made her mind up at that instant as Philip Manders walked away and she watched him disappear through the Market Hall entrance. Although she talked to Aunty Jo and her dad about his invitation, and although she prevaricated for several weeks before she went down to the offices of Barker & Bright to see him, Mary now knew where her immediate future lay. Would she like to work in and around the livestock market? Would she like to be involved with the numerous farm sales and auctions the firm was renowned for, and be paid for it? You bet your life she would!

CHAPTER SIX

Molly had followed the police car from the market to Chesterton police station. By the time she arrived, Billy had been taken down to the cells. The custody sergeant had listened to an account of Billy's arrest from the arresting officer and decided that, in spite of it being Saturday, he should seek advice from the Station chief inspector. By now, news had filtered through that Gary Radley was, indeed, dead.

"Where's my Billy?" Molly roared at the desk sergeant.

"He's in the cells at the minute," came the reply. "He's quite comfy and in good hands, so why don't you go home and ring us later? About 9 o'clock I'd suggest, we'll be able to tell you then whether he's been charged and if he has, what with."

"Yer listen to me, Constable," Molly was still roaring, "I'm not leaving here without him. I'm tekkin' him hum so as he can 'av a bath an' I'll put him into some clean clothes an' bring him back in the mornin'. He's been at work all day an' he's 'ad that shirt on fer a wik. If you think I'm leavin' him 'ere in that state you got another thing comin'!"

Molly's face was redder than ever, always perspiring, and her cheeks, her breasts and her upper arms all quivered at once as she continued her tirade.

"I'se met your sort afore, sat on yer arse in yer posh uniform. Bloody good days work ud kill yer, all bloody tay drinkin' an' clock watchin', that's all you'm good fer. Now I'm atellin' yer, go an fetch our Billy, or as sure as eggs is eggs, I'se comin' round that desk an', live or die, I'll smack thee, copper or no copper. I'll smack thee unmerciful I will, then yer can bloody well lock me up an all."

"Mrs Perkins," the sergeant began, "if it makes you feel any better you can shout your abuse as much as you like. I've heard it all before, dozens of times, and as for your threats, I'm ignoring them. Now, listen to me. Your son, Billy, has apparently been involved in an incident in Ampleford Market Hall in which a man was killed. I understand he was very actively involved, in fact. In the next couple of hours, there will be senior officers arriving here to talk to your Billy and decide the way forward. In the meantime, he's stopping here, in the cells, in police custody until decisions have been made. He isn't going home with you, or anywhere else with anyone else. Now, if you'll settle yourself down, I'll get a nice cup of tea brought up for you and I'll arrange with a lady officer to come up and explain things to you. You may get to see Billy in due course but I can't promise. Whatever happens I will personally make sure that you are escorted back to your home later in the evening and kept informed as to what is happening."

Molly calmed down, she gathered her grubby, voluminous skirts around her and settled down on a green, leather bench, which ran along one side of the police reception area. Her brain was muddled. Her instincts were aggressive, to fight verbally and physically, if necessary, in pursuit of Billy's welfare. On the other hand, something held her back from any further altercation with the sergeant. She remembered Mary Jones' words to Billy as he was loaded into the police car. "I'll come and see you directly, trust me and I'll see you very soon."

"That Mary's only seventeen," she thought, "but smart as paint, she'll know what to do and she'll be here in a while." The cup of tea was nice, the police station was warm and she settled herself down to wait. She looked at the station clock on the wall behind the desk – just after half past six. She could see through the windows – the snow was still swirling across the sky. Racked with worry and anxiety, she sat twiddling her fat grimy thumbs and waited.

Back at Crest Farm Cottage, Mary had hastily spilled the tragic story to her dad and Aunty Jo. Fifty yards away at the farmhouse, George Evans was engaged in similar dialogue with his brother, relating the facts as Mary had outlined them to him on their journey home.

"I had better go and see what it's all about," said Harry Evans, as he pulled on his overcoat and cap. "It strikes me that it was our cash tin the man snatched. Like it or not, we are at least indirectly involved so I'll go and find out what's happening."

By the time Harry Evans arrived at the police station things had moved on. It was now eight o'clock. Chief Inspector Williams had arrived and he immediately took control of the case. "We can hold him for two days without charge," he observed, "so there is no panic, but with all the evidence already at our disposal, I can see no reason why, providing he has a solicitor present, we cannot charge him with murder tomorrow morning. I will speak to the Chief Police Prosecutor as soon as possible and come back at ten o'clock tomorrow morning."

The custody sergeant now had the unenviable task of telling Molly that Billy must remain at the police station for the time being and that if she wished she could return with clean clothes and personal toiletry requirements at any time. Harry Evans was similarly informed – it was obvious his continued presence would serve no purpose, and as he left Mary and Aunty Jo came through the door only to be given the same advice. Mary's request to see Billy was refused but she did extract a promise from the sergeant that he would tell Billy she had been and that he would give him the chocolate bar she had brought for him, also, to assure him that she would be back tomorrow. At that, they all made their troubled ways back to Crest Farm.

It was Sunday; Inspector Williams had been unable to contact the Chief Police Prosecutor so nothing happened. Molly, Mary and Aunty Jo arrived at the police station at ten o'clock, having driven down in the old Morris Minor, only to be told they could have no access to Billy until the following day.

Molly had taken him some clean overalls, pants and socks, and a box filled with chicken sandwiches. Slowly, the gravity of Billy's situation was dawning on them all. On Monday morning things happened quickly. The court duty solicitor, one Mr McFarland, arrived to interview and advise Billy. Thirty minutes later, and following his discussions with the prosecutor, Chief Inspector Williams formally cautioned Billy and charged him with the murder of Gary Radley.

At two o'clock, Billy was loaded into a Black Maria and taken to Ampleford Magistrates' Court, where a bench of magistrates transferred the case to Chesterton Crown Court for a hearing in seven days' time. Billy was remanded in custody pending that hearing, and duly transported to Blackditch Prison, some thirty miles away.

Mary, Molly and Aunty Jo followed the Black Maria all the way to Blackditch Prison in the old Morris Minor. It was four thirty when they arrived. They had driven across the Fells in the gathering darkness, on snow covered roads. Having parked in the visitors' car park, they made their way to the Prison Visitors' Reception area and Mary explained to the reception clerk the reason for their presence.

She described their relationships to Billy Perkins, voicing their deep anxiety as to his plight, his vulnerability, and requested to be allowed to see him, to comfort and reassure him. The clerk, a dour middle aged man, told them to sit down and said he would make inquiries of the Prison Welfare Officer and whether she would see them.

"We ain't movin' til she does," spat Molly.

She was quickly hushed up by Aunty Jo saying, "Just be patient, Molly, you won't hurry these people, let's just see what happens."

After about thirty minutes, the Prison Welfare Officer did come to see them and escorted them through the maze of corridors which led to her office. She was an elderly, sixtyish, kindly lady, who quickly put them all at ease. She listened intently to their explanation of Billy's mental shortcomings, their deep concern for his welfare if he should be mixed with, or have any contact with, other inmates, also his need for constant supervision and instruction so that his everyday personal needs could be met. She spoke to them quietly yet firmly, and said at the outset that, to her, Billy's welfare was of paramount importance. Billy was in the process of being assessed as a new inmate and she would be conveying all the information they had given her to the staff in the induction office, explaining that all new arrivals had to pass through that department before placement in any other part of the prison.

She continued to explain to them that they could not see Billy out of visiting hours – two thirty until four o'clock daily – but that she would personally visit him as soon as he had been moved into his own room. She gave them further reassurance by outlining Billy's status in the prison. "You must understand, Billy is not a convicted criminal at this moment. He is not serving a prison sentence but is on remand. He is entitled to many concessions as a remand prisoner, and will almost certainly have his own room. You may rest easy that he is going to be given food, he will be warm, and all his toiletry needs will be attended to. Before you go, give me your telephone number. I will ring you tonight at around nine o'clock, after he has been accommodated and I have had a chance to see him."

They quickly realised there was nothing more to be gained by remaining at Blackditch Prison. Having voiced their gratitude for the comfort Mrs Bradbury had given them, and the obvious interest she had in Billy's welfare, they took their leave and drove back towards Ampleford and up to Crest Hill, arriving weary and drained at half past eight.

Mrs Bradbury did ring Molly at nine o'clock, "'E's had a shower, 'e's had a good dinner and 'e's in his own cell fast asleep, her told me. I feels a little bit 'appier now," was the message she passed on to Mary and Aunty Jo. "We'll see what tomorrer brings."

Molly and Mary did visit Billy the following day, although Aunty Jo's duties kept her in Ampleford and Mary was left with much explaining to do at school. Her reputation there meant that her story was readily accepted with much sympathy and understanding.

Billy was, indeed, fine and, apart from asking about twenty times, "When con I cum hum, Mom?" and throwing his clinging arms around her when she said, "It's time to go now, Bill," he seemed in quite good spirits. They all visited Billy again on the Saturday and promised to see him in court on Monday. In spite of Billy's apparent well-being, they all continued to lose sleep and endure periods of deep despair and desperate worry at Billy's situation.

Prior to the Monday hearing at Chesterton Crown Court, Mr McFarland, solicitor for Billy, had been in constant communication with the police prosecutor. Having studied the Crown's case against Billy, he indicated that he would be advising Billy to plead not guilty to the murder charge laid before him. "Absolutely no intent or pre-planning in this matter," he said. He also indicated that if offered the lesser charge of manslaughter, his advice would be to plead guilty. The deal was done. There would be no trial.

As soon as the hearing was opened on Monday morning, the police prosecutor sought leave to address the court and indicated to the judge the change in his position. He revealed the details of his discussions with the defendant's legal representative and declared that after much thought, he had come to agree with their arguments. The change of plea would expedite the matter through the court and save much legal wrangling and unnecessary expense.

The judge put the new charge to Billy. "How do you plead, Mr Perkins? Guilty or not guilty?" Billy turned in bewilderment to Mr McFarland, mouth agape but silent. "You plead guilty, Billy, you plead guilty now, don't you?"

Billy turned back to face the judge. "Guilty," was the sole word he whispered.

Witnesses came and witnesses went; market traders, policemen, ambulance men, a doctor and one, Bob Merrick: "Saw it all, I did, ker, ker, ker, kicked his head in he did, ker, kicked his bloody head in," he stammered.

"Thank you, Mr Merrick," said the judge. He turned to the court clerk. "I am mindful of the time, Mrs Buckley. How many more witnesses are there? If more than one, we might as well adjourn now and reconvene in the morning. If only one, we might as well finish the hearing."

"Only one, Your Honour."

"Call Mary Jones," the usher cried. Mary slid quietly into the courtroom and then into the witness box. She struggled to hide the nervous anxiety that was coursing through her and tried hard not to be overawed by her surroundings. The usher gave her a copy of the Bible and held up a card. She read the oath, quietly but clearly, swearing to tell the truth.

Mr McFarland, solicitor for Billy, questioned her closely about the events of that fateful, icy, Saturday evening. Mary could do little more than confirm the facts given to the court previously by Molly and the other witnesses. Mr McFarland then moved on to question Mary about her relationship with Billy. "How long have you known Billy Perkins, Miss Jones?" he asked.

"All my life," came the reply. "Billy and his mom are our neighbours from down the lane. We played in the fields when we were toddlers, three, four, five years old. We went to Ampleford Primary School. Billy was a bit slow somehow, and often the other kids would tease him because he hadn't got a dad and I used to stand up for him because I did not think it was fair. I used to tie his shoelaces up and put his coat on, things like that and, well, you see, Your Honour," she turned her head towards the judge, "I suppose, in a way, I grew to love him, like a brother, somehow. He didn't have a dad and I didn't have a mom. I did have Aunty Jo, of course, to look after me but I don't have a brother or a sister and ever since those days, those school days, I've always looked out for Billy and looked after him and somehow I always will." At the back of the court, Molly Perkins and Aunty Jo were reaching for their handkerchiefs.

Mary sensed that what she was saying was crucial. She sensed that the judge was listening with intense concentration to her every word and that her words were somehow, maybe, scratching at his emotions. She realised that if she did not seize this chance to defend Billy, it would be lost forever. As she spoke out, her voice went a little higher and a little louder. She did not wait to be questioned and, with trembling lips, she erupted into an outburst of wanton emotion. "Sir, Your Worship, you mustn't lock Billy away, you mustn't. You'll turn him into a caged animal – you'll destroy him. I know that man died but it was an accident. Billy just did what his mom told him to. Billy might never hit anyone again as long as he lives. You must understand that he doesn't think about things except whether he's hungry or full, whether he's wet or dry. Sir, I beg you to understand, Billy's not a lunatic, he's just not quite like a normal person, he just needs help and support and understanding. Thank you, thank you, sir, Your Worship."

She had run out of words as she grabbed the witness box with her hands, and her shoulders slumped with relief. Her head tipped forward, her soft auburn hair falling down around her face. She felt an empty relief as she realised that in those brief, trembling moments, she had revealed so much about her own life as well as Billy's. The period of silence that followed was total. Not a rustle of paper, not a cough or a sneeze to be heard, a silence you could cut with a knife. Clearing his throat, the judge took charge of his court once more.

"Miss Jones, er, er, thank you for your evidence and for your insight into the defendant's mental capacity, I am grateful." In truth, the sheer spontaneity of Mary's emotional outburst had moved him greatly. The prosecutor declined to cross examine Mary and with her cheeks a little flushed and her heart pounding, Mary moved from the witness box to the rear of the court. Billy's haunted eyes followed her every inch of the way. He had grasped the gist of her outburst and simply gazed at her with a forlorn look of adoration. She half smiled, half grimaced at him, putting her fingers under her chin, signing him to put his shoulders back and keep his chin up.

Eventually, the judge put his hand up to his mouth, coughed and cleared his throat.

He proceeded, "Mr Perkins, you have come before this court today, charged with the manslaughter of one Gary Radley. You have pleaded guilty to that charge with a submission from your solicitor for clemency, based on diminished responsibility as a result of your mental incapacity. I am not going to sentence you today. Matters will be adjourned for six weeks' time, pending the production of a psychiatric report, which will be organised by the Probation Service. I am going to grant you conditional bail to return to your home, because I do not believe you pose any immediate threat to the general public. Your bail is subject to the following conditions: you must co-operate in every way with the production of the report; you will be bailed to your home address and subject to a full twenty-four hour curfew. This means that if the police call to check, you must always be there, at all times.

"Finally, you must be back at the court on the appointed date and at the appointed time for a sentencing hearing. Is that all fully understood?"

Billy's solicitor rose. "Thank you, My Lord. Be sure that everything will be fully explained to Mr Perkins."

There was great relief from everyone connected with Billy: Mary, Molly, Aunty Jo, and the many market traders who had attended to lend their support to Billy's case. Billy was going home – for the time being anyway. There was, however, still the cloud of another day in court hanging darkly over all their heads. In six short weeks, they would be back again, with the distinct possibility of Billy going to prison.

Mary was finishing her final year at Chesterton High School, busy with her exams, and looking forward to July, when she would start work at the offices of Barker and Bright.

The six weeks soon flashed by, with Billy oblivious to the possible fate he was facing. Molly and Aunty Jo had many pangs of anxiety and deep forebodings as to what the future held. The Evans family kept their distance, unhindering, yet unhelpful. The appointed day arrived. They all turned up at court – at ten o'clock. Billy stood in the dock, a picture of bewilderment.

The judge, in all his berobed and bewigged splendour, gave his customary cough and proceeded. "I am about to address Mr Perkins and all his relatives and friends. I have studied at great length both the psychiatric report and an additional report provided by the Probation Service. These reports reveal that Billy Perkins has very serious limitations in all aspects of life that require any mental application. He has a very short memory span, recalling very little that has occurred more than an hour ago. His deficiency in life skills is so severe that it is quite obvious he will never be able to live independently without constant care and close supervision. He will always be unable to handle and deal with money, to use public transport, to go shopping or to provide for his own personal needs. In addition, he is completely illiterate and innumerate. Fortunately, Billy Perkins has no physical shortcomings. He is capable of long hours of sustained physical labour, work that is productive and of a good standard. However, even with this, he requires close and constant supervision."

He continued, addressing Billy directly, "As part of any sentencing exercise, it is my job to consider three things above all. There must be appropriate retribution, punishment for the crime that has been committed. I must be satisfied that the sentence provides public protection from further offending and, where possible, I should impose a sentence that contains elements of rehabilitation. The reports I have read indicate that any period of incarceration in any sort of institution, penal or otherwise, would be of little help to you or anyone else. I believe that, closely supervised, you pose little or no threat to the general public. It is my intention to subject you to a three year curfew and supervision order. You must remain at the property known as Half Crest Farm. With the exception of serious, urgent medical appointments, you must remain only at that property at all times. You are, in effect, imprisoned in your own domain. You should all know that the Probation Service will closely supervise and observe Mr Perkins throughout this sentence, and any breach of the curfew imposed will result in a quick return to court and a re-sentencing exercise, which would almost certainly mean a term of imprisonment. I will conclude by placing on record my observation of the importance of the friendship shown to Billy Perkins by his close neighbours, Mary Jones and Barbara Jones, particularly the former. Without the evidence given to this court by Mary Jones six weeks ago, and without my belief that she will continue to support the defendant, I do not believe the sentence I have passed today would be either workable or appropriate."

The relief on Crest Hill was total. Gone were the dreadful, gut wrenching, gnawing pangs of anxiety suffered by them all. Gone was the sleepless tossing and turning in the small hours. Gone was the dread of the impending court hearings and the fears of Billy's possible fate. Billy was home in his own bed, permanently, not just for the time being but for good.

There were murmurings from the Radley family that Billy had 'got away with it'.

Idle threats were made that came to nothing. They knew that the vast majority of local people were of the opinion that Gary Radley, the thief, had got what he deserved. They also knew that following any form of retribution against Billy, the finger of suspicion would be pointed straight in their direction. Peace reigned, everyone got quietly on with their lives.

Aunty Jo and Dick decided to change the old Morris Minor, after twelve years of reliable service. Once again George Baylis at Ampleford Motors was the provider – he came up with a nearly new, bottle green Hillman Estate car which they could easily afford. Although Aunty Jo struggled with the lump in her throat as she handed over the keys of her beloved Morris Minor, she soon bonded with the new Hillman, recognising the practical advantages and extra space the estate car provided. Mary was learning to drive, and Billy's curfew order posed little or no hardship to anyone – he didn't go out much anyway. Life carried on.

CHAPTER SEVEN

So it was that in that summer of 1959, Mary's young life began to take shape. She was duly interviewed by Philip Manders the week before she left school and engaged as a junior clerk. Although she had worked hard for her exams, in truth Philip Manders had his mind set on employing her whether her results were good, bad or indifferent. He had recognised her practical skills and common sense, anything else would be a bonus. When her results did come along in August they were excellent – top grade passes in all subjects.

She had opened the envelope with a little indifference when Aunty Jo handed it to her on her return from work. By then she had been at Barker and Bright's for some five weeks or so and was loving it.

"Oh, our Mary," began Aunty Jo, "I hope you don't regret taking that job at the market office and wish you had gone for something a bit better. You've got the brains, you know."

Mary would have none of it. "I am more than happy where I am at the moment. Everyone is so kind and the work is varied and interesting. I'm loving it, really loving it, so don't worry, Aunty, if I ever think it's wrong I'll tell you."

Mary's days were stimulating and varied, sometimes at her desk in the small office, sometimes helping book in stock at the livestock market, sometimes on telephone duties, and sometimes travelling with Mr Philip, as she had styled him, to arrange and conduct farm auctions. The farmers and drovers gently teased her and made her laugh, but her obvious affinity with the cattle and sheep on market days, and the quiet professional way she conducted herself around the market, attracted their respect and admiration.

"You've got a right tidy wench there, Mr Philip, smart as paint and sharp as a tack her is," was a typical comment when Mary was out of earshot. "You wants to look after her, pretty little thing too, ain't her?"

Philip Manders didn't need telling. He was inwardly quite proud of himself, having spotted Mary's qualities and secured her services for the firm. He had no intention of spoiling her but would certainly be 'looking after' her and nurturing the obvious talents she possessed. The fact that she was pretty was irrelevant but in the overall scheme of things, the fact that a member of staff was 'pretty' was nothing to be ashamed of.

Mary had been working at Barker's for a year and, as was her habit on Wednesday lunchtimes, when the weather was kind, she left the office and strolled down to the town park. She found an empty bench, overlooking the lake and there, in the shade of the ancient chestnut trees, she would enjoy the fresh air and sunshine. She would eat her sandwich and apple, away from the busy office, the telephones and general buzz of commercial activity that she had to endure on most other days. Wednesdays were relatively quiet. On Wednesdays, she had a proper lunch hour, free and uninterrupted. Mary had walked deep into the park to the far side of the lake. She glanced at her watch – quarter past one. "I must start back at quarter to two," she noted. Conscientious Mary, mustn't be late. She was, she thought, a lone visitor to the park. She listened to the singing birds and watched the dappling shadows ripple across the grass, as the sun pierced the waving leafy branches high above her head.

Mary turned, and suddenly she was there, sitting at the other end of the bench. Mary had not seen her until that very instant. Mary had not heard her. An icy quiver shivered rapidly up Mary's spine. There was something eerie, something scary about the instant manifestation of the gypsy lady who now shared her seat. Where had she come from and with such stealth?

"Did oi startle you, Ducky?" she said – deep gravelly words that could have been uttered by a man.

Mary sat in frozen silence. She knew instantly her bench mate was a gypsy – her toothless crone-like features, deeply wrinkled brown leathery skin, coal black eyes, grimy fingernails, and a gown and shawl as black as the crows that squabbled and screeched in the nearby treetops. She wore shabby men's shoes, the brightly coloured bead necklace around her neck being her sole gesture to femininity. She smelt like a gypsy – Mary's nostrils were filled with the odours of wet, rotting leaves, wood smoke, ditches and drains all mixed together to produce a pungent, acrid, dark scent – unique, not retchingly offensive, but indicative of a human body not often tended with soap and water.

"Now, listen right careful, Duckie," she growled, "I'se got a story to tell yer, a story as will bring yer vantage, if yer duz wot I sez. Hundred years ago an' more, my old ma was a scullery maid up at Slopeham Grange. Big 'ouse, big estate then it wuz. Well, one night, it set light and burned to the ground. Some on 'em perished in the fire, Ma got 'erself out, an' in the confusion, 'er snook a little painting under 'er cloak. Pretty soon arter, 'er took up wi' a Gypsy lad, Jakey Harris an' ad me – pretty quick as I understands it. 'Er couldn't do nuthin' wi' the paintin' cos erd've gone te jail for thievin', or so 'er thought. Later on still, me Pa took the picture to Chesterton an' sold it to a little antique shop, down the end of the cobble lane, for two quid, more than enuf to live on fer a month then it woz. Now, jus yer listen careful, me Duckie," she said, advice she needn't have bothered to give as Mary was now hanging on to every raspy word. She continued, "Now get yer up te Chesterton, my wench, an' be sure an' buy that little picture. It's still there, twenty pounds it is. Jus' goo an get it, it's summat you'll never rue – an' don't ax me ow I knows these things, I jus duz."

"But why are you telling me these things?" Mary asked. "Why me?"

"Duckie, there ent much yer old Granny Harris don't know about. Yer bin real good to Billy Perkins, yer 'as, uncommon good – I knows. An' allus 'member, Duckie, us folks looks forrud as well as backud. I reckon yer'l allus look out fer 'im, an let's just say we allus looks arter air own. Doon't ax no more now, jus do wot I sez."

Mary watched her hobble away down the path. She watched her for a few brief seconds and then took a fleeting glance at her watch to check the time. When her eyes looked up to view the path again, she was no more. Like her entrance, her exit was instantaneous, inexplicable, and that chilling shiver travelled once more up Mary's spine.

Time to go back to the office, her mind a turmoil of imaginings at what she had heard. She quickly dismissed the thought that she may have been dreaming, as her nostrils snatched again the unmistakable odours the gypsy had brought with her. Mary's nose was the sole confirmation of the gypsy's manifestation – she could be seen and heard no more but Mary could still smell her. She hurried back to the office in deep thought and, for now, she determined to say nothing – to anyone.

Mary settled herself back behind her desk and set about the afternoon's tasks. After the turmoil of the previous day's livestock auction, Wednesday was sorting out day. The office was small but pleasantly situated on the first floor, overlooking the sprawling rooftops of Georgian Ampleford. Mary was part of a team of five coping with the Wednesday work, preparing invoices to send out to the previous day's buyers, settlement statements and cheques for the many vendors who had brought their stock to market. Her four workmates were all considerably older than Mary, married ladies who had all been with Barker and Bright for many years. There were good working relationships between this little team of clerks, and in spite of Philip Manders' efforts to allot specific duties to specific people, they always slid back into 'all mucking in together' mode. It worked, they were happy – the work was done properly and on time, so generally he left them to get on with it without interference. One person with one specific task, however, was Mary. Every afternoon at half past three she made the tea. Mary was the office junior and in spite of her capabilities, tradition ruled. She didn't mind, she treated remarks such as 'best tea we've ever had since you came, Mary' with the mild contempt they deserved.

"Oh yes, I'll bet you've been saying that to everyone else who's made the tea in the last twenty years," she would reply with a wry smile. As she attended to her tea making duty on this particular Wednesday afternoon, her mind was awash with the images and reflections that her lunchtime encounter in the park had generated. She completed her task, returning dutifully to the office with the tray replete with six steaming cups.

Philip Manders worked in a downstairs office but always joined the General Office ladies for his afternoon cuppa. Finally, as they all sipped their tea and nibbled their biscuits, Mary's patience gave way. "Anyone ever heard of Slopeham Grange in these parts?" she enquired.

"My God! That's a bit of history if you like," Philip Manders retorted very quickly. "Bit of local legend and folklore that place is. Burnt down, sometime in the 1830s I think."

None of Mary's office colleagues had any knowledge of Slopeham Grange and one immediately asked Mary why she had asked the question.

"Well, I bumped into an old lady in the park at lunchtime. We got talking about local things and she mentioned it – she mentioned a fire actually – but I didn't realise she was going back so far."

Philip Manders continued, "Huge fire it was, apparently the Wilberforce family and many servants perished. No Fire Brigades then, they all lined up and passed buckets of water from the lake, didn't do much good though. Place was crammed with valuable artefacts and furniture, or so the story goes."

By now, Mary's brain was working overtime – 1830s, that's nearly one hundred and thirty years ago. She was sure she had heard the gypsy clearly. "I was born soon arter" were words she recalled, "pretty soon arter the fire er met up with Jakey Harris". The words were clearly imprinted in Mary's brain. She calculated and recalculated a dozen times, her mind in turmoil as she strained to find an explanation for her lunchtime experience. However much she twisted the years, she came to the conclusion that the gypsy, Granny Harris as she had styled herself, was at least 125 years old. The icy shivers returned once more to Mary's spine. She was fearful and apprehensive as to what she might be letting herself in for if she followed the gypsy's advice. Where might it all lead and with what consequences? She divulged no more of her lunchtime experience. "I just found it interesting, that's all," she said guardedly, bringing the tea break conversation to a close, but not before Philip Manders had promised to lend her a book of local history.

"It's all in there," he said, "a whole chapter on the Wilberforce family, I think. Wiped them all out, as I recall, something like eight hundred years they had been up there before the fire."

As good as his word, Philip Manders handed the local history book over to Mary the following morning. She waited until lunchtime before spending fifteen minutes or so flicking over the pages and gazing at the sepia photographs. There was Ampleford High Street at the end of the nineteenth century, ponies and floats parked outside the shops, grocers and butchers wearing white aprons, bowler hats and boaters, and lady shoppers in bonnets and long flowing gowns. There were old photographs of the Town Hall, the Cottage Hospital and the concrete horse trough at the top of the High Street – still there to this day, now brimming with tumbling flowers. As she continued, her attention was suddenly caught by an old print, a drawing really. At the bottom it read, 'Slopeham Grange, circa 1820, destroyed by fire in 1832, detail taken from the County Archives Department'. The print depicted a building that was impressive to say the least, much bigger than anything in the locality at the present day. There were dozens of mullioned windows and a vast main entrance door at the top of an impressive flight of curved steps. The door was heavily carved and adorned with iron hinges and handles. The upper storeys bore gargoyles and at roof level the whole structure was castellated with turrets at each corner.

Mary took the book home and during the evening spent an hour or so poring over its contents. She found virtually nothing other than the old print of Slopeham Grange that was of any interest. Details of the fire were sparse; there were no accounts of fatalities or destruction of artefacts, just a brief note that lives were lost. There was, however, a further photograph of an old print depicting a man in military uniform, sword dangling from his waist, an Admiral's hat under his crooked arm, entitled 'The Right Honourable Walter Wilberforce, Admiral of the Fleet'. Alongside the text was a coat of arms, two lions rampant facing each other, and the motto Semper Fidelis.

Mary returned the book to Philip Manders the following day. She was confused, her mind undecided as she pondered whether to share the entire story with all the details of her dalliance with the gypsy either with Mr Philip, or perhaps Aunty Jo. She decided against the latter. 'Aunty Jo will just poo-hoo it, I know she will,' she thought. 'Don't believe in all that mumbo jumbo, don't get involved,' that's what she'll say. She decided to keep quiet for the time being but she knew that, at some stage soon, she would share the details of the gypsy's appearance and the fascinating information she had imparted. Her opportunity came earlier than she thought.

A few days later Philip Manders asked her into his office and told her that he wanted her to accompany him on a visit to a farm some distance away, on the other side of Chesterton. The visit was to take place in seven days' time and its purpose was to discuss the impending sale of both the property and the live and dead stock contained therein. The landowner, John Biggins, had no heirs and now into his middle sixties had decided to call it a day.

"It's just an initial visit to discuss terms and possible values with him, and generally get a feeling for things. I need someone to take notes – full use for your shorthand there, I thought. I will need to refer to those notes before I write formally to him, outlining our arrangements."

It made little difference to Mary. Interesting indeed, and she was happy that Mr Philip trusted her discretion in matters that were obviously confidential but, really, it was just another day, another job – her mind was elsewhere. As she sat quietly at home in the evening, it occurred to her that if she was going through Chesterton in a week's time, why not locate the antique shop and seek out the painting described in the gypsy's story. Her mind was made up. The following day, as she entered Mr Philip's office with his morning coffee, she asked if he could spare a minute – he could.

"Now, I expect this is all going to sound a bit far fetched," she began. She proceeded to explain why she had been so interested in Slopeham Grange. She related the gypsy's tale and revealed the burning curiosity that now consumed her. "I've simply got to find that antique shop and just see if there is such an article there. Do you think we might find time to have a quick look next Thursday when we come back through Chesterton? It could be a wild goose chase but it should only take twenty minutes or so."

"Do you know, Mary, I think I know that shop, antique shop you call it, piled up with the biggest load of junk you'll ever see. Of course we'll call in. I am just as curious as you are now – wonder what we'll find?"

The next few days came and went. The visit to the farm was uneventful if tinged with a little sadness. "Been on this place fifty years, you know, came here with my old dad," John Biggins began. "Been here ever since, end of an era I suppose, still, all things come to an end and we should have a nice few quid to keep us going. It would all be different if we had kids but you can't put the clock back, that's for sure."

Meanwhile, Mary was constantly taking sly peeps at her watch. As they said their farewells she glanced again, four o'clock. 'We'll be back in Chesterton before half past,' she thought, time enough to accomplish what was, for Mary, the main objective of her day. She was desperate to satisfy her curiosity, to put an end to the wranglings in her mind, to find out once and for all if there was any substance in the old gypsy's haunting tale. Soon she would know.

Sure enough, it was little more than twenty minutes before they were driving into Chesterton. Mr Philip pulled into the car park of the Green Dragon Inn at the Cathedral end of the city. He parked the car with the words, "Come on then, little lady, let's go and see if we can sort your story out." He steered Mary into a side street. "This leads eventually into the Cathedral Gardens and, if memory serves me right, the shop you have described is on the corner at the very bottom." The side road was cobblestoned and some of the buildings were black and white beamed, of Tudor origin. The upper storeys overhung the thoroughfare and were decked with typical latticed windows. They strolled for a hundred yards or more until they reached the end of the road, and there it was – on the corner as Mr Philip had predicted. It had three bowed lattice windows. The two outer ones were glazed with the old bull's eye glass from the early nineteenth century, with timber frames screaming out for urgent restoration. The centre window was also latticed but the glass was modern, giving an easy view of the interior of the shop. A sign above the central window read simply, 'Olden Times', and a small sign on the inside of the central window said, 'Browsers Welcome'. The entrance door was in the side alley.

"Come on then, let's go panning for gold," said Mr Philip. Mary took a deep breath as they entered the shop, the door giving an almighty warning clang as it closed behind them.

"Afternoon to you both, looking for anything in particular, are we?" The words came from a little man, probably in his seventies, balding head with side whiskers, rimless glasses perched on his nose and with a heavy gold chain hanging across his waistcoat, on the end of which was a gold pocket watch. He pulled the watch carefully from his waistcoat and took a brief glance before saying, "Don't close till five thirty so you've plenty of time."

They had actually got little more than half an hour as Mary piped up, "We just want to have a little look around if that's alright."

"Carry on, my dear, carry on," came his reply.

Philip had been right, it was a shop full of old junk. There were old earthenware pitchers and vases with £2 labels on them, umpteen horse brasses hanging from the beams, a suit of armour, and brass warming pans of various sizes. A stuffed barn owl in a glass dome gazed down on them, and there was a stuffed pike in a glass case, with a brass plate attached saying, 'Taken from Crest Pool, Ampleford, March 1866, Weight 32lb 7oz'. Mary eagerly pointed this out to Mr Philip as they both knew Crest Pool. They picked their way through the clutter of old tables, chairs, chaise-longues and sideboards, and came into a smaller rear room, the walls of which were hanging with numerous ancient oil paintings, local prints and porcelain plates. As they peered at the display of paraphernalia hanging before them, Mary suddenly took a little gasp, "Oh, my God," she exclaimed, her hand rising to her mouth, unbelieving at what her eyes had landed on. Her tummy knotted slightly as she said, "That's it, that must be it. Look, there's the dove in the tree looking down, there's the military man standing by a bench with his family seated on the bench. That's what she said, that's what she described," she said breathlessly, "and look, a coat of arms, the same as in that local book you lent me, 'Semper Fidelis', I remember it."

The article she had spotted was occupying a particularly dingy corner of the room. No light fell on it and the top of the frame was thick with dust. Philip Manders looked closely and carefully for probably a minute or more at the porcelain plaque Mary had identified. It was about twelve inches by fourteen inches and set in a frame of warm sepia coloured ivory.

"I'm no expert," he said at last, "but I would say the quality of the painting is extremely fine. There is something about it that just oozes quality. It's twenty pounds so it's up to you. It's a gamble, and let's be honest, if it turns out to be bog standard ordinary, at least you have got something to hang on the wall and you will have a bit of a story to tell about it. Have you got twenty pounds with you?" She had. "Come on then, no more messing, let's get it bought and get off home." Philip carefully lifted the plaque from its position off the wall and they moved back towards the main part of the shop.

"We would like to purchase this illustrated plaque if we may," Philip said. "Just perfect for an empty wall in my office," he lied.

"I will find a suitable box for it," the little man said. "You won't be very pleased if you break it on the way home. It's porcelain you know." He continued, "That's been here for sixty years to my knowledge. I inherited this place from my father, who inherited it from his uncle – that's three generations, possibly been here for a hundred years or more. I ought to get some of these things re-valued really, but you know how it is, finding the time and taking the trouble, with everything else there is to do."

'Lazy bugger,' thought Philip. "Can we have a receipt please?" he said. "Put it in the name of Mary Jones, if you don't mind."

Mary handed her four crisp, white, five pound notes over, and the old man, having placed the plaque into a box which was now tucked under Philip's arm, proceeded to write out the receipt. At that moment, Mary half turned to glance through the shop window on to the street outside. She gasped, her body froze, her stomach somersaulting with a million butterflies. There looking into the shop was the unmistakable face of the gypsy, the deep wrinkles, the toothless, crone-like features she had seen a few weeks ago in the park, the black clothes and the bright bead necklace around her neck. Her face seemed to twist into a suppressed grin as their eyes met. The spectre Mary was beholding was, at that instant, etched into her brain, a vision that would remain there for the rest of her life. The gypsy turned and quickly started to hobble along the street, retracing the path that Mary and Philip had walked some thirty minutes before.

She caught Mr Philip's arm, "Look," she gasped, "that's her, the gypsy lady, that's her, quick, quick, I must follow her." She hurtled through the shop door and stared in disbelief along the whole length of the roadway ahead. She was gone, not a clue, except it was there, the smell. The same dark acrid odours she had last encountered in the park now snatched at her nostrils.

By now, Mr Philip had joined her outside. "Tell me, tell me," she pleaded, "Can you smell her? She was right here just seconds ago!"

"Smells like a blocked drain to me," he replied. "Not unusual. Mary, you know, you have gone as white as a sheet. We have got what we came for, now let's get back to the car. I will buy you a tot of something in the Green Dragon and then take you home."

Mary caught his arm – the experience of the last three minutes had shaken her visibly. The memories of that haunting face, that twisted grin, would be with her forever more. They walked the short distance back to the car in silence. The light was starting to fade as Philip locked the box containing the plaque in the boot of his car. "Come on, let's go and have that drink I promised."

Mary wasn't used to pubs but the inside of the Green Dragon Inn was particularly nice – all old beams, hanging with trusses of hops, flagstone floors, an inglenook, and a roaring log fire. It was cosy. Mary had no idea what drink to ask for until her eyes lit upon some bottles of Babycham. She had been given one of those at Christmas and she quite liked it, especially the little baby reindeer on the label. They found a quiet corner in the almost deserted pub and sat down.

"Do you know, Mary, back there you really did look as though you had seen a ghost?"

"I know you are a bit sceptical about this," Mary replied. "I think you are teasing me a little but I did see the gypsy lady outside that shop, and her smell, the same as in the park, it was there."

"Let's go over this again, let's recap. Exactly what did she say to you in the park?" Philip enquired.

"She said I had been very kind to Billy Perkins and that 'us folk always looks after our own'. She said we can see forwards as well as backwards and that if I bought the painting it would be to my advantage. Aunty Jo has told me that most folk believe Billy's dad was a gypsy but I don't care really. If that painting is some sort of reward for looking out for Billy then it is so unnecessary. I don't want rewards."

Mr Philip took up the conversation. "Mary, at the moment that painting is worth twenty pounds, not a penny more. When we get it valued I will not be surprised if it turns out to be worth quite a lot more. We've got to wait and see but if you have had a bit of good fortune, stop punishing yourself, accept it, and enjoy it! Life has a way of balancing these things up sometimes – it's called 'taking the rough with the smooth', and if this is a bit of the smooth, so be it." He continued, "I must say, I do worry slightly about how much this Billy Perkins thing may affect your future life, particularly when anything happens to his mother."

Mary looked horrified, aghast. "Mr Philip, calling in to see Billy four or five times a week doesn't affect my life in any way whatsoever, nor my work."

"Well, certainly not your work, I wasn't suggesting that," replied Mr Philip. He could see that he had touched a nerve. Mary had been involved in similar discussions with Aunty Jo.

Mary continued, "If anyone is suggesting I stop going to see Billy, they can forget it. If you could see his eyes twinkle when he spots me you might understand. He practically sparkles, he jumps up and down, both feet off the ground and then follows me, so closely, like a shadow if you like. My visits mean more to him than anything else in the world and to stop going would be so cruel. I have to be honest, after being associated with him for so many years, I probably take as much out of it as he does. Let's face it, if he was my blood brother, or sister for that matter, no one would expect me to turn my back on him. Quite the reverse I suspect. Without being disrespectful to Billy, to ask me to cut him out of my life is like asking me to burn my old teddy bear I've had since I was five years old, or asking Grandad to have his dog put to sleep, it's just not going to happen."

Philip had heard enough. "Good heavens, it's half past six, your folk will be worrying and it's all my fault, dragging you into a pub. Come on, let's go home. I will put the painting in the office safe for you if you wish and we will start to look into it more thoroughly after the weekend."

The following few days were uneventful. Philip Manders had a brief word with Mary to say that during the next couple of weeks he was expecting a visit from a man called Harry Hayden. He explained that once a year Barker and Bright conducted an Antique and Fine Arts Auction in their local saleroom. The auction was in conjunction with Harry Hayden's firm, Wooley, Mitton and Jenks, a substantial estate agency from the neighbouring county.

"I know Harry well," Mr Philip explained to her. "He is a fine art expert of some renown, and we find it better to link up with him for our own sale. His firm has more knowledge and expertise in that field and thus, once a year, we are giving local people the chance to buy or sell their artefacts without travelling far. When he is here I will ask him to view your painting, Mary. I would trust his advice if I were you. Personally I can't wait to hear what he's got to say."

Some ten days later, Harry Hayden duly arrived at the offices of Barker and Bright: a small bespectacled man in his late forties, with a neatly trimmed beard, balding head and wearing what looked to be a regimental or university tie. Having finished his business with Philip Manders and completed the detailed arrangements for their joint sale in a month's time, Philip said, "Harry, will you just cast your eye over a little painting? It belongs to Mary Jones, one of our secretaries. It's in our safe – I think I should call Mary in to listen to your opinions and perhaps you can advise her."

"No problem," came his reply. Mary was duly invited into the office. Introductions completed, Philip proceeded to lift the painting from the large office safe and placed it on his desk, facing Harry Hayden. Harry pulled his chair closer to the desk, pushed his spectacles back a little and peered closely at the porcelain plaque. He picked it up and held it so that it caught the light from a side window.

"Wow!" he exclaimed, "this is beautiful. Where in God's name has this come from?" He continued in his clipped, cut glass accent, "The art work is so fine, look at the leaves on that tree, the features on those faces, the control of the light as the sun's rays come shining through that foliage, it is simply superb. Certainly at worst nineteenth century, probably earlier. I don't expect you have noticed but woven into the blades of grass in the bottom right hand corner there is a cleverly hidden monogram, RWT, I think. Now that will help someone to place it," he said as he pointed out the initials to Mary. "Where did you get it from?" he enquired.

"I bought it from an antique shop in Chesterton, on the advice of a well-wisher," she replied.

"How much?" Mary looked directly and appealingly at Philip.

"Go on, tell him," said Philip.

"Twenty pounds," the words spilled from her mouth.

"Look," Harry Hayden began, "you haven't bought it, you've begged it. It's certainly worth more than that, miles more. I can't value it exactly, far more research is needed and you must consult people who know more about these things than I do." He looked at Philip Manders. "Philip, this is a London job. In my opinion, Christie's or Sotheby's, or someone similar, should view this. You will possibly be able to send them photographs to begin with, but at some stage you are going to have to take it up there. Photographs are useful but only up to a point – they wouldn't give you a final valuation without actually seeing it. They may give you ball park figures perhaps but whatever you decide to do, I can tell you without fear of contradiction that you have a valuable piece of fine art on your hands and that any trouble you go to will be well worth your while."

Harry departed but not before promising to phone Philip the following morning with the contact names and telephone numbers of his London acquaintances and, good as his word, he did exactly that. Philip Manders spoke at length to Mary the following afternoon. The main thrust of the conversation was to explain to her that research into the painting and the valuation of it was a time consuming and expensive exercise. Photographs were needed, and letters, probably several, would need to be exchanged, and eventually a journey to London and back was very much on the cards.

"What you must be sure of, Mary, is that you really want to sell this article – turn it into hard cash. Furthermore, in fairness to my partners here, I will have to charge a commission for my time and out-of-pocket expenses. As an employee here, these will be extremely favourable for you but really, the main thing is, what do you want to do?"

"Sell it," replied Mary, "as soon as possible. There's something weird and spooky about the whole thing and to be honest, I can't wait to get rid of it and put it all behind me. Definitely, sell it."

"Okay," replied Philip. "I am going to be very busy for the next week or so and then we have got this Antique Sale, and then the farm sale for John Biggins so it might be two or three weeks before I can make any real progress, but in the meantime I will arrange for the photography – that will get the ball rolling. I must say, Mary, I am just a little excited for you but let's wait and see."

CHAPTER EIGHT

As the next few months unfolded, events would develop that were to prove monumental in the shaping of the future lives of Mary and her family.

She was quite content to let Philip Manders ferret away in his own time with regard to the painting and had told him not to disclose anything until matters were complete. "I would rather not know until everything is concluded. Don't tell me until you have the full story, whatever the outcome."

"Well," said Philip, "if that's the way you want it, so be it. I always thought the female sex were a curious, nosey, impatient lot – you must be the exception!"

Nothing, however, could have prepared Mary for the stunning news she was to be given two weeks later from a completely different source.

It was her habit to drop in to see Molly and Billy on her way home from work. She would have a cup of tea, a little chat, give Billy a hug, and be on her way in about half an hour. One day before Mary left, Molly spoke up. "Listen, when yer calls next Thursday, Mr Wilkes, my solicitor is going to be here. I jus' wants to be sure yer'll be cummin' and that yer'll stop a little bit longer 'cos I wants yer to witness some changes as I'm mekkin ter me will, and what I wants to 'appen when I'm gone."

"Yes, I'll be here," said Mary. "Aunty Jo will drop me off at the usual time." As she left to walk the half mile up the hill and home, she concluded that she was going to be asked to witness Molly's will.

As promised, at five fifteen on the following Thursday afternoon, Aunty Jo dropped Mary off at Molly's place. Mr Wilkes' green Rover car was parked in the yard and Mary admired it as she walked by.

"It's only me," she called, having tapped the kitchen door and let herself in. "Come on, Mary, we bin waitin' for yer." Molly, Mr Wilkes and Billy were sat at the kitchen table which was strewn with documents and files. "Sit yer down, it'll not take long and I'll mek yer a cup o' tay directly." Mary sat down.

"Right, what do you want me to do? I have never done anything remotely like this before," she said.

"Well, actually, there isn't anything for you to do, so to speak." The words came from Mr Wilkes, a hefty red-faced, middle-aged man with wavy, fair hair. Mr Wilkes had been family solicitor to Molly for over twenty years and whilst, in the normal course of things, she had little need for his services, she trusted him. Mr Wilkes continued, "You see, Mary, I will try to explain. Molly came to see me some months ago and asked for my advice regarding the inheritance of her estate, particularly the farm. I gave her that advice but insisted she gave matters long and careful thought before she jumped, so to speak. Molly came back to me last week having asked me to prepare a new will, which she duly signed. It was witnessed by my secretary and is now in safekeeping at my office, so to speak. I think Molly should now tell you why you are here – the key point is you are a beneficiary in that will, so to speak."

'God above,' thought Mary, 'how many more times will he say *so to speak*.'

"You mean Molly has left me something in her will?" enquired Mary.

150

"I'se left yer the farm, lock, stock and barrel. When anythin' 'appens ter me, it's goin' to you, Mary, that's what I wants, and that's what I'se done."

Mary sat rigid, stunned into silence. Her lips moved to say something but the words would not come out, and her face became flushed as she tried to analyse the implications of the words she had just heard. Eventually she murmured, "You can't do that, you mustn't. What about Billy?"

"Listen, our little Mary," replied Molly, "now listen good 'cos I ent very good at words. There's a nice sum of money, £15,000 to be exact, gone into trust for Billy. Mr Wilkes an' you are the trustees. It can't be spent, only for Billy's welfare, medical treatment and the like, and then only if you and Mr Wilkes agrees on the need fer it, so I'm happy that he ent goin' to be penniless or put into some home of some sort, so that's all sorted. Now, that leaves the farm. What could Billy do with it? Look at him, he don't know what day it is, bless 'im." She took a deep breath. "Mary, let me tell yer, I'll never forget how you've bin with Billy over the years, ever since you was both running about in nappies, the pair of yer, and what you did down in that courtroom last year will live with me 'till I takes me last breath. You was always there, through all the pain and worry, but there's summat else as well. I ent very good at sayin' these sort o' things but I loves yer like yer wuz one o' me own, and now I'se done this I feels real good about it."

Mr Wilkes piped up, "Mary, I did advise Molly against this course of action. After all, you will probably get married and may decide to move miles away, so to speak. Furthermore, there is no legal obligation in Molly's bequest that leaves you with any responsibility for Billy's welfare. Molly's position is that she regards you as family and I must say, having met you this afternoon for the first time, I have shifted my opinions somewhat, so to speak. Anyway, it's all signed and sealed now and I suspect that, given the passage of time, you and I," he looked directly at Mary, "will be meeting again at some stage. Please be assured if you need any advice or support at any time, my door is always open, so to speak." Mr Wilkes said his goodbyes and departed. Billy watched him through the kitchen window as he left the yard and sped down the hill in the green Rover.

Mary left soon after, but not before saying to Molly, "I don't know what to say about what you have done, Molly. Never in my wildest dreams did I expect anything like this to happen to me. It's going to take some time for it to sink in and it's given me so much to think about. I am so grateful to you."

"Grateful, grateful? Grateful's on the other foot if you axed me, darlin'. I know what I'se dun is right, now let's leave it at that."

By the time Mary arrived back at the cottage, the clock had moved on to past six thirty. "You're late," remarked Aunty Jo. Dick and Grandad were sat at the kitchen table, having just finished their tea. "You don't usually stop at Billy's for that long – it's not his birthday or anything, is it?"

Mary could not contain herself. "Listen, I have got some news for all of you. Something happened down at Molly's this afternoon that's just knocked me sideways. I honestly don't know whether to be excited, or worried, or what." Mary sat down at the table with Dick and Jack, and Aunty Jo joined them. "I'm not sure whether I've dreamt the last hour or so but when I got to Molly's, Mr Wilkes, her solicitor, was there. Well, it seems as though Molly's left me in her will – she's left me the farm, the land, the house, the buildings, the lot. When she dies she wants me to have it all."

Aunty Jo put her hand up to her mouth as she stammered, "Dear God alive, what will this mean to us all?"

"Not a lot for a long time yet," replied Mary. "Molly's as sound as a pound for a good few years yet."

"Whatever it means it doesn't sound like bad news to me," said Mary's dad. "No, it aint bad news, that's for sure." Both he and Aunty Jo had become resigned to the fact that Billy Perkins would always play some part in Mary's life.

Jack, now in his eighties, and always a man of few words, spoke out. "It's wonderful. I don't expect I will ever live to see you there but it's a lovely little place, good land, watered and well-drained. You'll have your hands full to cope with that lot, our Mary, but, my God, you'm a lucky little lady, that's fer sure."

"Listen," said Mary, "I do not want anyone to know about this, absolutely no-one, including the Evans'. Let's keep it strictly in the family and let's face it, it's not going to change any of our lives for a long time yet."

"Oh, for pity's sake, no, don't let them up at the farm know anything about it," said Aunty Jo. "I've got to say, our Mary, whilst I've always been a bit worried about the way you have always sort of mothered Billy Perkins, I've always thought that there was something very caring, and Christian and nice about it. Most folks have to wait to go to heaven to get the reward for their good deeds but it looks as though you are going to get yours down here."

As the weeks rolled by, things went on quite normally at the cottage. It was as though there was some unwritten pact that no-one would talk about Mary's prospective inheritance – it would not change any of their lives for quite some time and so it was stowed away in the recesses of their minds. Grandad Jack spent most of his life in his old ladder-backed chair by the fire in the kitchen. Dick would take

Peggy, the collie, with him when he started work in the mornings. She would have a good run round the farmyard and return at breakfast time, and have another run round later on in the afternoon. She spent the rest of her time lying no more than a yard from Jack's chair. Peggy was the last of Jack's legendary collies – she would not be mated, the line was over.

By now, farming was changing dramatically as mechanisation and new techniques had brought about a revolution in the industry. Combine harvesters now gathered the summer harvest, with grain silos appearing on the farm for storage. Grass was made into silage to feed the stock through the winter months. It was much less chancy than haymaking which depended on dry, sunny weather. Whilst a little hay was made for the young calves and lambs, ninety per cent of the grass was made into silage. Dick had to learn new skills, how to drive new machinery, and he had to adapt to the activities required by the new methods. He did so quite readily as he could see the enormous advantages they brought. The farm was much less at the mercy of the weather, and the mechanisation of the actual milking of the cows made it so much quicker and easier.

Aunty Jo carried on with her duties as the district nurse. She was now approaching her middle fifties, with a wealth of nursing and midwifery experience behind her. "I've got another good ten years in me yet," she often said. "Driving the car instead of all that biking is the best thing that ever happened for me," was another of her comments. It had to be said, she was greatly admired by Dr Powell and everyone at the local surgery. Furthermore, to the people of Ampleford and surrounding areas, she was a local treasure. By this time, she was receiving lots of help with all the household chores from Mary. Mary was at work in

Ampleford every weekday and did most of the shopping for their domestic needs. In addition she would often spend Saturdays baking cakes and pies, washing and cleaning.

Aunty Jo was so grateful. "Mary, you really are a good girl, you have given me a chance to put my feet up for an hour and listen to *Mrs Dale's Diary* on the wireless. I'll make a cup of tea first, though, and we'll try one of these little cakes you've made."

Mary was hankering to pass her driving test. Her dad had given her a few lessons in the Hillman and she yearned for the independence her own car would bring. She would often daydream about her own car – it would come quicker than she imagined!

Mary was invited into Philip's office. It was Monday morning, half past eleven, start of a new week with loads of work to get on with. Mary always looked forward to the Tuesday livestock market, with all its hustle and bustle, and generally relished the challenges that each new week brought.

"Sit down, Mary," Philip began, "now you told me not to give you any news of your painting until my enquiries were completed, and I had solid information as to its value and its history. Well, after four weeks, I have got some news for you. I received a letter this morning confirming the information I first received by telephone last week. I decided to put the matter in the hands of Thomas Whatley and Partners, a very highly regarded firm of Antique and Fine Art dealers. Their offices are in Bond Street, and they also have an office in New York. As you will see from the letter, the painting has got to be taken to London – I think the best thing to do is for you to read it, Mary." He handed the two page letter across his desk with the words, "Take your time."

She noted the golden, gilded, embossed heading at the top of the page, and started to read: 'Subject to further close examination and scrutiny, initials R.W.T. almost certainly those of Robert Walter Turton, a distinguished painter of the late eighteenth century, specialising in portraits, oils on porcelain.' Mary was speed reading, eagerly scanning the lines in front of her. 'Subject is certainly a member of the Wilberforce family of Slopeham Grange, Ampleford – records of eight such painted plaques, all thought lost in the great fire of 1832. Your client's discovery is very exciting. You have said your client wants to sell; recommend our October auction. We will advertise the sale of this artefact globally.'

Mary gasped as her eyes fell upon the last paragraph, her brain struggling to believe what she was reading – 'In our considered opinion, the item should have a reserve price of £10,000 (ten thousand pounds). We would expect it to be much sought after and we would hope it will make somewhat more. We would suggest that it is insured for that sum.'

For the second time in a month or so, Philip watched Mary's face drain white.

"I don't know what to say," were Mary's first words. "It doesn't seem real, or right somehow. It doesn't feel as though that painting or that money belongs to me, or even that it should belong to me. I don't seem to have done anything to deserve it. Really, it's all so weird."

"Mary, I am absolutely thrilled for you, relish your good fortune," Philip said. "I've told you before, life has a way of evening things up somehow and you haven't always been lucky, have you?" Philip had in mind the loss of her mother when she was five years old. "When the time comes, if you wish, I can introduce you to people who will invest the money for you, for your future and so on."

"Will I be able to buy one of those new Austin Minis with some of it?" Mary enquired.

Philip rocked with laughter, "That's more like it, little Mary. You'll be able to buy twenty Minis if you want to, but perhaps one will do to start."

The next couple of months were uneventful, and quickly rolled by. Philip had duly delivered the painting by hand to London, involving him in a full day's travelling, by car and taxi, to the offices of Messrs. Whatley in Bond Street, but Mary did not go with him. In truth, she could not wait to see the back of it, to get the whole experience behind her. She often thought about the two occasions when she had witnessed the sudden manifestation and subsequent disappearance of the gypsy. Whilst it did not play on her mind unduly, she still looked back on the experiences as eerie, chilling, and not something she had enjoyed. She also wondered whether she had seen the last of her.

Philip received the news of the painting's sale in late October, firstly by telephone, and then by letter with a cheque enclosed. It had been sold to an American buyer for a staggering £12,000. Messrs. Whatley's commission of five percent, and further out-of-pocket expenses, reduced this by £900, whilst Barker's input was calculated by Philip as being £250. Thus Mary finished up with a cheque from her employer for £10,850.

Even when she was given the cheque by Philip, she still could not believe it. "I keep thinking I am going to wake up in a minute and find out it has all been a dream. This sort of thing just doesn't happen in real life." She gazed at the cheque at length. "I haven't got the slightest idea what to do with this sort of money," she said eventually. "It still doesn't seem right somehow."

"Now, listen," said Philip, "I have been taking advice on your behalf from several sources. You can rest assured that all these people are very professional men and that none of your business affairs will leak out – these matters will not be divulged to anyone. The general consensus of the opinions I have collected is that your best interests will be served by the following: firstly, you can put the £850 into your bank account – that will take care of that new Austin Mini you are longing for; then it is proposed that you invest £5,000 in the Mellshire Building Society – they will add £250 bonus premium to that immediately. Your money will be as safe as possible and will earn you 5% interest annually, thereby increasing the capital sum by £250 or more every year. Furthermore, the money will be readily accessible. Finally, there is an estate of really nice, modern, detached houses being built on the outskirts of the town. It is called Broadlands Park. They are being priced at just under £2,500 each and we at Barker's are the selling agent, so why don't we get your money into a couple of those? I will personally manage the letting of them to respectable clients, and you should achieve a rental income of at least £500 a year. We at Barker's will collect and transfer the rents straight into your building society account. Furthermore, those houses will be worth a lot more than that one day, I'll wager."

"Look," said Mary, "I am so grateful for everything you are doing for me so please don't take this the wrong way, but I must discuss all this with Dad and Aunty Jo first. At the moment they know nothing at all about the painting, about the sale of it, or the gypsy, or anything, and it's going to come as a bit of a shock. Could you put your advice down in writing for me, please? I really must come clean with them as soon as possible."

'God,' thought Philip, 'I wouldn't mind being a fly on the wall when this news hits them.'

"No problem," he said, "I will type it up myself in the morning and, in the meantime, my advice to you, Mary, is for heaven's sake stop torturing yourself and just enjoy your good fortune."

For Mary's part, she couldn't wait to get everything off her chest. For some time now she had been suffering pangs of guilt that these things had been going on in her life for nearly a year, and she had said nothing to her Dad and Aunty Jo. The following day, as promised, Philip handed Mary a note setting out his recommendations for the investments he had outlined.

After a busy day in the office, she arrived home at the cottage at six o'clock, having popped in to see Billy for a few minutes. She hardly waited to take her coat off. Dick, Aunty Jo and Grandad were all taking their ease looking forward to listening to *The Archers*, waiting for Mary's arrival, and eagerly anticipating the beef casserole that was coddling away on the range, filling the kitchen with the delicious aroma of good old fashioned country cooking.

"Before we sit up to eat," started Mary, "I have got something to tell you all – something has been happening to me in the last few months. I haven't said anything before because I wasn't sure how it would all turn out."

"Oh, my God, you haven't got mixed up with a man, have you?" gasped Aunty Jo.

"Certainly not," replied Mary. "You would have known months ago if I had." She proceeded to regale the story of her meeting with the gypsy, and all the details of everything that had followed – her trip to Chesterton with Philip to buy the painting, the appraisal of it by Harry Hayden, and its subsequent sale in London. "I am really sorry I haven't said anything about this before but I just thought it would worry you all and, at the end, there might have been nothing in it, but that's it, and that is what Mr Philip thinks I should do with the money. I do trust him and I am sure he would not give me bad advice."

They all sat dumbstruck, bewildered and confused. Grandad, who had worked his entire life and never had more than £400 in cash in his hand, could simply not comprehend the sums of money he had heard mentioned.

Dick's response was to say, "I hope you are not going to get into any trouble, our Mary. That painting was stolen in the first place and there is something about it all that seems too good to be true. I just hope it's all above board, that's all."

Mary quickly reassured him that, at the very outset, she had discussed the legitimacy of it all with Mr Philip. He had taken advice and had assured her the object was rightfully hers – he had often used the words 'sold and bought in good faith'. She had her receipt from 'Olden Times' and any misdemeanour that had taken place over a hundred years ago ceased to be relevant.

"This all comes back to the Billy Perkins' thing, doesn't it?" piped up Aunty Jo.

"Yes, I suppose it does," said Mary, her eyes brimming with tears, "but I haven't asked for any of this and now it seems to be upsetting you all and putting a wedge between us. I would rather give it all away to some charity than let that happen." She wiped her eyes with the back of her hand.

Aunty Jo continued, "Coming so soon after the business of Molly's will, it's a bit hard to understand, our Mary. In my experience, it's one thing to be short of money and poor, it's another thing to have just enough to live a decent, happy life, but it's something else totally different to have far too much. I don't think I've ever known rich folk who were really, really happy and, let's face it, our Mary, it's only a couple of years since you left school and that's the bracket you are moving into."

Aunty Jo looked across at Mary's crumpled features and it suddenly hit her. Mary was deeply upset by it all – she had done nothing to deserve to be upset like this, and that perhaps she should look at the situation differently. Whatever had happened must be God's will, she thought. He must have determined that this is what should be. Maybe only good would come out of this and maybe they should all be more positive, rejoice even, at Mary's good fortune. She stood up and beckoned Mary towards her. She hugged her for all she was worth, saying, "Mary, nothing in the world is going to put a wedge between us, nothing – certainly not a pile of money!" They were both crying by now and comforted each other for several minutes before drying their eyes and sitting down again. Having gained their composure, Mary urged that outside of the house nothing be said on the matter that might reach the ears of other folk. Exactly as before, regarding Molly's will, silence was the order of the day.

And so it unfolded. Philip invested Mary's newfound wealth exactly as he had suggested. Mr Wilkes, Molly's solicitor, handled all the legal requirements for the purchase of the houses, and having been told the whole story, said, "Well, I thought I had heard it all in the last twenty years, but this takes the biscuit – a disappearing gypsy, an antique shop, a forgotten painting worth so much money. Following on from Molly Perkins' bequest, whatever next? Perhaps you will win the football pools. Anyway, good luck to you, Mary. My advice is to take care of it. There is an old saying 'make it first and make it last'. In the meantime just enjoy all the security you now have, so to speak."

CHAPTER NINE

Mary bought her new Austin Mini, a blue one – she loved it! She loved the independence it gave her. Having passed her driving test at the first attempt, she didn't have to ask Aunty Jo to pick her up and take her everywhere. With this newfound freedom, she embraced the spirit of the swinging sixties and all that brought with it. She collected the records of the Platters and the Beach Boys, and saw the Beatles burst into the pop world. She went to the cinema with some of her old school chums and saw Cliff Richard in *Summer Holiday*, Gordon MacRae in *Oklahoma*, and Doris Day in *Calamity Jane*. She loved them all. She also joined the Ampleford Young Farmers' Club. They met every Tuesday night in the Village Hall. She joined enthusiastically into their activities and looked forward to the weekly meetings when a guest speaker would deliver a forty minute speech to them. One week it might be a senior ranking policeman, or a fire officer. It might be someone from the world of education or someone with a medical background. Mary always found the talks interesting and stimulating, giving her an insight into the way other people lived their lives.

By now, Mary was twenty, a very pretty and attractive young lady, with an infectious smile and giggle. She was not short of male admirers, nor a host of offers to take her out. Whilst many of the young farmers seemed to be pairing off, even getting married, no-one came along who really made it happen for Mary. The Young Farmers' monthly Saturday night hops, when they would dance, jive, and twist the night away, provided a natural atmosphere for boys and girls to form attachments. Mary was often asked if she would like a lift home, or if she would like to go outside, or if she would like to go to the pictures when a new film was on at the Plaza. Her answers to these questions were invariably, "I've got my own car, thank you", or simply "No", or "I'll let you know". She had never yet felt strongly enough about anyone to want any permanent involvement or commitment. She had seen other girls' lives suddenly change when they started courting. Boyfriends became jealous, and resented any activities that did not include them.

"They are frightened to move," she said one night when chatting to Aunty Jo in the kitchen. "I'm free and easy and that's how it's going to stay."

"Hmm, we'll see," said Aunty Jo a little cynically. "There is someone for everyone I was told, but look at me. You're a lot prettier than I was, though, so just keep an open mind. One thing's for sure, you'll be a good catch for someone one day."

Strictly behind her back, and out of earshot, Mary's attitude towards boys had, rather cruelly, resulted in her being referred to as 'the Virgin Mary'. If she had known, she wouldn't have cared much anyway. One Tuesday morning she was checking in stock at the market, when an old farmer, with a twinkle in his eye, tried his hand at teasing her about her unattached status, "How is it you 'ent got a bloke yet, Mary, pretty wench like you?"

"'Cos I have met too many like you, Fred, that's why!" came her sharp retort.

The arrival of the new Mini had been noted by Elizabeth Evans up at the farm. "How the hell can she afford that? She's been at work in an office for less than two years, and there she is running about in a brand new £500 car. Probably on tick I wouldn't be surprised." The words came from a face twisted with envy.

Her father replied, "It would surprise me. That family are very careful with their money, you know." The fact that Elizabeth roared round the lanes in her green MG sports car did cross his mind but he left it at that.

Billy was progressing nicely through his curfew order. By now, the probation officer only called once a month and, with only six months to go, he told Molly that if they applied to the court for an early release from the sentence, he would support the application. With Mary's help, Molly contacted Mr McFarland, Billy's solicitor, and the application was successfully made. Billy hadn't really missed going out but at least they could now take him shopping and down to the market again, and Mary was determined to take him to the Young Farmers' Club.

At the next meeting, Mary asked if she could say a few words to the gathered throng, about forty boys and girls aged between sixteen and twenty-five. At the end of the meeting the chairman, David Nokes, tapped the table and announced that Mary Jones wanted to say a few words.

Mary stood up, cleared her throat with a little cough, and began, "It's about a new member I would like to bring to our meetings – it's Billy Perkins. Some of you know him from school or from the market. He's retarded. Mentally, he's never going to get any better but he loves the company of people his own age. I have thought for a little while that if you would allow him to join the club, it would be marvellous stimulation for him. He is quite harmless and I will personally keep a close eye on him, and if he does ever offend anyone, I will take him home straight away. I will just say that at times he has been treated as a bit of a clown

– someone to tease and poke fun at, so to speak." She paused and thought to herself, 'Oh, God, now I'm saying it!' Mary continued, "I would be very disappointed if that happened here, that's all really, Mr Chairman, and thank you for listening to me."

As she sat down a voice rang out from the back of the room, "Killed someone a couple of years ago, didn't he?"

Mary jumped to her feet. "Mr Chairman, it's not fair to bring that up. He's served his sentence. The man that died was a thief, and Billy's never been in any trouble before or since." Mary's face was, by now, quite flushed and her voice had trembled.

David Nokes had noted Mary's anger and moved quickly to quell the situation. "Can I suggest, as your club leader, that we allow Billy Perkins to attend the next four meetings on probation? If he settles in, we can make him a member in due course."

There was a general consensus that this was a good idea. It was put to the vote and passed without objection.

Billy did go to the next four meetings – he loved it. He stayed close to Mary and just kept grinning at everyone. He was no trouble at all and jumped into Mary's car eagerly every Tuesday evening, having been bathed and dressed by his mom. He shone like a new pin, and in his new jeans and a Fair Isle pullover someone in the village had knitted for his birthday, he was as presentable as any of the other club members. After the four weeks' probationary period was over, Mary just kept taking him. Nobody had voiced any objection to his continued presence and so she did not see any point in bringing the matter up. Billy was soon to become quite a star at the Young Farmers' Club in an activity no-one had anticipated.

At the summer County Show, the Young Farmers' Clubs from all over Mellshire would have an annual convention, a sort of jamboree. The whole thing took place in their own designated area and was hugely competitive. A silver cup was presented to the club that amassed the most points. There were stock judging competitions, with competitors required to place pigs, sheep and cattle, usually three of each, in their correct order of excellence. They then had to stand before the judges and explain the reasons for their placings. There was a hurdle-making competition, and a trailer reversing contest between a slalom-like arrangement of posts. The girls baked cakes and took along homemade jam and chutneys, and in addition there was an inter-club tug o' war contest. This was conducted on a knockout basis, leading up to the semi-finals, and ultimately to a final which took place in the Grand Ring before several hundred spectators.

Enter Billy Perkins, ace member of the Ampleford team. If Ampleford could win the tug o' war, they would win the County Cup for the first time in ten years. Billy was number one in the team of eight, right at the front. They had been practising at recent Tuesday night meetings on the green outside the village hall and it soon became obvious that Billy had immense strength, power and stamina, both in his legs and upper body. It took him a little while to master the rules, and on the first two occasions he was invited to join in, he ignored the instruction 'stop pulling'. Billy kept heaving away for all he was worth, and with every vein and muscle in his body strained to bursting point, he proceeded to pull the opposition several yards across the grass by himself.

"For Christ's sake, somebody, tell that prat to stop pulling," came the plea. He eventually did, but there and then it was decided to put him in the club team at the County Show.

"It's like trying to pull a brick shithouse over when he's on t'other side," was a typical attempt to describe Billy's talent for tug o' war.

By the time the County Show came round, Billy had mastered the rules and was fitted up with a huge pair of brown boots without laces. This enabled him to dig a ridge in the ground with his heels and increase the power he was able to exert on the rope. The final came along. The Ampleford team entered the main ring to cheers from the hundreds of spectators surrounding the area. The opposition, a team from Limbury, had won the contest for the previous two years. Billy's reputation had gone before him.

Limbury members were muttering, "We've got no chance pulling against that ginger ape they've got at the front."

"More like the missing fucking link than a human being he is."

The contest went according to form, best of three pulls – Ampleford 2 Limbury 0. Billy was hoisted shoulder high and carried from the ring amidst much rejoicing and to the strains of 'he's a jolly good fellow, and so say all of us'. David Nokes, the club chairman, was so proud. For the club to have won the County Cup under his leadership meant so much to him.

Later in the afternoon he said, "Do you know, Mary, it strikes me that if you hadn't brought Billy Perkins down to the club in the first place, we would not have won that cup, and that's not taking anything away from everyone else who competed today. The fact is he made the difference at the end. It's funny sometimes how things work out."

Mary wasn't quite so sure that all the euphoria and hullaballoo was entirely in Billy's best interest until she dropped him back at home later that evening. As she pulled up in Molly's yard she said, "Go on in then, me old mate, be a good lad for your mom. You've had quite a day, that's for sure."

Billy did not normally put words together apart from, "I wants me dinner," or "What shall I do next?" Now, however, he turned to Mary and with lips quivering said, "That's my bestest, bestest day ever, Mair. My bestest day in my 'ole life." He left the car and walked towards the farmhouse. As he turned and waved, Mary gave a little toot on the horn and sped up the hill to home. She swallowed hard on the lump in her throat and enjoyed the warm feelings sweeping over her. Billy had enjoyed the day of his life and Mary loved that!

For the little family in Crest Farm Cottage, the next twelve months were relatively uneventful. Aunty Jo continued to hurry and scurry round the town with her district nurse's responsibilities. Dick, who was the finest example of a loyal, trustworthy, English countryman, was now technically under the control of Elizabeth Evans who seemed content, however, to allow her father to direct Dick and the rest of the staff. Her main preoccupation continued to be with her horses, and for now the farm could take care of itself. Grandad had discovered television. A black and white set was installed as a joint Christmas present, a family treat, paid for out of the common pot.

Mary's job at Barker's had now, after three years, developed to a level where she was virtually the office manager. The older women had homes and husbands and children, and were all part-timers. They recognised Mary's industrious talents and were quite content to adopt subservient roles.

Mary's investments were thriving, still a secret from everyone except her family, Philip Manders and her advisers. Her houses had appreciated by fifty per cent in the first year and her building society account now stood at over £6,000. There were, alas, clouds on the horizon. Things would happen that would bring great anxiety and pain to them all, but they would cope.

CHAPTER TEN

Grandad was the first to hear of Dick's accident. An ambulance, with siren screaming, came hurtling up the lane and turned into Crest Farm drive. He had heard it approaching and left his chair, moving towards the kitchen window to see what was happening. He saw it entering the farmyard some hundred yards away and then lost sight of it as it disappeared into the complex of barns and general farm buildings that made up Crest Farm. Some twenty minutes later he watched it return along the drive and turn back down Crest Hill, its siren still at full blast. 'Wonder what that's all about?' he thought. Ten minutes later Grandad heard a knock on the door. He opened it to reveal Harry Evans on the step.

"I've got some bad news, Jack," he began. "Dick has had a rather nasty accident up in the middle barn there. He was trying to move the bale elevator into a corner out of the way, and somehow it toppled over. The top end of it fell across his right leg, and his right foot and ankle are badly crushed. He lost consciousness for a few minutes. The ambulance people have injected him to relieve the pain and taken him to Chesterton General Hospital. He's lost a quantity of blood but he was talking to one of them as they loaded him up, so I think he's going to be alright. They have got our 'phone number, the farm number that is, so if I hear anything I will let you know."

It was half past three in the afternoon. It would be more than two hours before Mary or Dick's sister, Barbara, came home from work. Jack Berry was now over eighty years of age but he was far from senile and quickly reasoned that he should contact Mary or Aunty Jo and inform them of Dick's misfortune. He scratched about the set of shelves in the front hall where the telephone was located and uncovered a local directory. He peered at the pages – there it was, Barker and Bright. Shakily he dialled the number and asked to speak to Mary Jones. She responded almost immediately.

"What's wrong, Grandad?" she asked. She knew that Grandad would not be ringing her at the office unless he had something pretty serious to tell her.

"It's your Dad, he's had an accident up at the farm and Mr Evans says he's gone to Chesterton General in an ambulance, about twenty minutes ago. I should let your Aunty know if I were you."

"Ok, Grandad, leave it to me, try not to worry too much, and I'll see you soon." Mary knocked on Philip's office door, opened it and pushed her head round the corner. "Sorry to barge in," she began, "I have just had a call from Grandad. Apparently Dad has had an accident at the farm and he's gone to hospital in an ambulance. Is it alright if I shoot off an hour early? The post's gone off and everything is tidy."

"Good God, yes, get down there and see what's going on. I hope it is nothing too bad." Philip advised her to take care and mind the rush hour traffic.

Mary drove the few miles to Chesterton General as quickly as safety would allow. On arrival she was told that at that very moment Dick was having an emergency operation on his right leg. She was assured that his injuries were not life-threatening and that as soon as the operation was over, the surgeon would speak with her. She settled down in the waiting area, having been given a cup of tea and warned that it could be an hour or two before her dad left the operating theatre. Before leaving work, she had telephoned Dr Powell's surgery and left a message for Aunty Jo, revealing what had happened, and that she was going to Chesterton General as fast as possible. She was assured that the message would be given to Nurse Jones as soon as she returned from her rounds. As good as their word, the message was passed on and Aunty Jo speedily followed in Mary's wake, arriving at Chesterton General at five forty-five, about an hour after Mary. It was barely five minutes after Aunty Jo's arrival that a hospital sister came into the waiting area and escorted them to Dr Pullman's office. The doctor was a slightly built bespectacled man with sharp features, black hair and a small moustache.

"Now let's sort you out," he began, "I understand that you are Mr Jones' only daughter, indeed only child." He was looking at Mary as he said this. "And you are his sister." He had turned to look at Aunty Jo and noticed her district nurse's uniform. "I have to tell you that whilst Mr Jones is basically alright, and without any threat to his life, we have had no alternative other than to amputate the lower part of his right leg, some little way below his knee. I have been given no details of his accident, only that it happened on a farm. Whatever crashed down on to the lower leg, ankle and foot has completely smashed that area beyond any hope of repair. Your father, your brother, is now in a side ward and receiving close, intensive care as he wakes up from the anaesthetic. He will not be in any great pain as this is being controlled, but he is going to be in a state of great shock and extreme trauma for some days ahead and I would expect him to remain in hospital for several weeks. Our major concern is to keep him free from infection and to that end he will remain isolated in his own room."

Aunty Jo was sat to Mary's left and she reached across with her right hand to hold Mary's arm in a gesture of comfort.

"When can we see Dad?" asked Mary.

"Well, there's not much point at the moment. I doubt if he will be awake for another hour or so, and then he will be fairly groggy and sickly for some hours. I would suggest that tomorrow afternoon will be the most sensible. I will instruct the ward sister to tell him you have been here, and that you know exactly what has happened."

"What does the future hold for Dad?" was Mary's next question.

"Everything will be done to ensure that he is able to live as normal a life as possible and he will certainly be fitted with an artificial leg. With a great deal of practice and physiotherapy, I am certain he will, in time, walk quite perfectly but it will be slow progress. You may draw some comfort from history – I am thinking of Douglas Bader who flew fighter planes in the RAF with two tin legs. For now, let's get your dad through the next few weeks and in a position to come home. He will probably be on crutches for some time but basically healthy and reasonably mobile."

They drove their separate ways home and told Grandad the grim news of Dick's accident. The mood in the cottage was sombre. They all wondered how the accident had happened and, whilst they had deep, stomach-churning anxieties about Dick's circumstances, there was the feeling that it could have been a lot worse.

"We know he's lost half his leg, let's be thankful he did not lose his life," said Aunty Jo.

They all went down to see Dick on the following evening. He was sat up in his bed and, although deathly white, he had eaten some of his dinner and was able to talk to them at length about the accident and how events had unfolded. With the onset of modern methods, the bale elevator had not been used for several years – it was in the way and Dick had decided to push it to a position where it would be less of a nuisance. It was mounted on a set of wheels and there was a metal pin on a chain that allowed adjustment in the height and angle of the track. As he had moved it along, inch by inch, the metal pin had jiggled its way free. Dick had then moved to the front of the machine and directly below it. He was trying to replace the safety pin when the force of his efforts caused the whole thing to topple and ultimately crash down. He told them that he tried desperately to scramble away but that he lost his footing.

"Another couple of feet," he said, "and I would have been in the clear. Now I'm in this bloody mess!"

Mary and Aunty Jo visited Dick every day, together when possible and if not, they went separately. Grandad went with them at the weekends and together they watched the slow but solid recovery he was making. He came home five weeks after his accident, by then quite nimble and lively on his crutches, and fully able to wash and dress himself and move around the cottage with ease. It would be another couple of months before he would be fitted with his artificial leg (peg leg he called it), and in the meantime, given the nature of his work, any thought of returning to the farm was out of the question.

Harry Evans, now nearing his eightieth birthday, had been to the cottage on several occasions to enquire about Dick's progress, and had visited him once at the hospital. The bale elevator was cut up for scrap, and to patch over the gap in the workforce caused by Dick's absence, Elizabeth's friend, Michael Mason, had moved into the farmhouse and taken over many of the tasks previously undertaken by Dick.

By now, Elizabeth and Michael Mason were living together, and over the previous three years had, between them, changed the whole strategy and business activity at Crest Farm. Everything about the place that was required to enhance the facilities for the horses was swallowed up – buildings, acreage, manpower and capital. The poultry were gone, the pigs were gone, the milking cows and beef cattle were no more. The sheep remained to graze the grassland and the higher ground, and most of the land not required for the horses was planted with corn to be harvested as a cash crop. In fairness to Elizabeth, she had built up a sizeable clientele of people using the farm as a livery facility for their horses, either their own or perhaps their child's pony. The income from this, however, even together with sales of corn and lambs, did not come anywhere near to making up the shortfall in the sales of milk, eggs and beef. There was money coming in from training fees, provided by a couple of owners who had entrusted the care of their point-to-pointers to Elizabeth and Michael, and the occasional prize money when they had a winner, but overall the financial performance of Crest Farm had deteriorated considerably. From being a highly profitable mixed working farm, it had become a playground for the wealthy that, month on month and year on year, lost money.

Harry Evans had watched it all happen with increasing dismay. He had witnessed the gradual break up of his life's work to satisfy his daughter's voracious obsession with horses. By now, he was too old and not legally entitled to do anything about it. He didn't even see the annual financial results, or the monthly bank statements. If he had, he would have seen that the cash balances had disappeared, to be replaced by an overdraft, and that the valuable farmland was the subject of a debenture required by the bank to secure the borrowing.

Elizabeth had regular conversations with her mother and Gerald de Beau and they would reassure her that she was really very wealthy, pointing out the value of the land and the houses that she owned. After one such discussion, her mother's parting shot was, "For God's sake, Elizabeth, if a ten thousand pound overdraft is worrying you, why don't you sell something – a bit of land for instance, or even that cottage at the end of the drive?"

The seed was planted and for several weeks she pondered her options. A letter from the bank brought matters to a head. The bank account balance had, for several weeks, been a thousand pounds or more over its agreed limit, and the branch manager was requesting Elizabeth to make an appointment to see him so that matters could be sorted out and the future of the business clarified. The appointment was made and the meeting, a rather icy affair, took place. Elizabeth was full of reassurance and optimism that the operation at Crest Farm, now mainly based on horses, would soon be showing a healthy profit. The bank manager, whilst taking comfort from the securities he held, was not convinced. Elizabeth suggested that it might be possible to sell off some of her assets and thereby clear maybe all, or at least part of the overdraft. He welcomed the idea with some degree of eagerness.

"That sounds like an excellent way forward and I do urge you to give it great consideration," he said.

As Elizabeth drove home, her mind was made up. Crest Farm Cottage was performing absolutely no positive function in her business activities – it contributed nothing. It was, in her eyes, a rent free home for an employee who was disabled and unlikely to return to do any sort of work for at least another six months, and even then she wondered how he would fit in. In addition, there was an ex-employee in his eighties, Dick's sister earning a healthy salary as a nurse, and Elizabeth's main irritation, Mary. She had not forgotten that Mary had more than likely seen her in somewhat compromising circumstances all those years before and moreover, she was deeply jealous of Mary – jealous of her popularity in the town, particularly with the farming community, and jealous of her position with Barker and Bright, and the respect she commanded from anyone who had dealings with her.

Elizabeth knew what she must do – evict Dick Jones and his family from the cottage and sell it for the best price possible.

"I'm running a business, for God's sake, not a housing charity," she reasoned, "and they will get a council house with ease if they ask."

Had she known of Mary's true financial situation, and of her prospects, she would probably have thrown them out that very night. She satisfied herself with the delivery of a letter asking Dick and Mary to visit the farm at 7 o'clock the following evening to discuss some important business. She did not really have to include Mary in the invitation but there was a streak of malice in her mind and she saw it as an opportunity to wreak some twisted revenge for the advantage she felt Mary had over her.

'She'll soon see her true position in the scheme of things,' she thought. 'She'll be back firmly in her place, where she belongs.'

Dick and Mary duly presented themselves at the farmhouse at 7 o'clock the following evening. Dick was still on his crutches. They were invited into the big kitchen and remained standing just inside the door. Mary quietly admired the views from the large window which looked out over Ampleford and the surrounding area – from that elevation it all looked so serene, a picture of great beauty. Elizabeth was sat at the table looking somewhat official, and had a quantity of papers and documents in front of her, giving the impression that she had been studying them.

She began, "I will come straight to the point. I have instructed our solicitor to serve you notice that it is our intention to repossess the cottage you are living in. It is a business decision. You and your family have been living there, rent-free, for many years. The cottage is a valuable asset that is contributing nothing to our business, and it is our intention to sell it and use the capital generated to further develop the rest of the farm, create more employment and so on. We are giving you three months to be out, which I think is quite generous. You should receive the solicitor's letter in the next couple of days but I felt it better to forewarn you personally of its contents." She looked into Mary's face which had not creased or cracked in any way. "Go on, cry, you little bitch," Elizabeth's mind was screaming, "go on, break down or something." Harry Evans was nowhere to be seen. He didn't even know what was going on.

Mary stared directly into Elizabeth's face and maintained steely-eyed contact as she replied, "Miss Evans, I believe there is another side to the way things have been at Crest Farm. For two generations my family have given your family total loyalty and honest commitment to their daily work. Your talk of rent-free accommodation is a distortion. The fact that no rent has been paid has been reflected in the weekly wage they have earned. It is true that at the moment, through tragic circumstances, my family are unable to contribute in any way towards the daily activities at the farm, but my father's present situation was caused by an accident here on the farm whilst pursuing his daily tasks. You could have suggested that it may be appropriate that we pay some rent for the cottage but," she took a deep breath, "you have chosen to throw us out, to make us homeless and in doing so, probably committed Grandad to an early grave."

Elizabeth's reply was short. "I have no intention of bandying words with the likes of you. You know where you stand and so I'll bid you both goodnight."

Mary would have liked to run back to the cottage, but she adjusted her pace to suit the limitations of her dad.

When they arrived and broke the news to Aunty Jo and Grandad, Aunty Jo's hand went to her mouth. "Oh, my God, whatever now, whatever next," she exclaimed.

Dick put his head in his hands. "That's the end of my life now, for sure," he said in a voice full of anguish. "What is there left for me?"

Mary quickly realised that she must take control of the situation. "Talk like that will do us no good at all. Of course your life's not over, Dad, it's just going to change, that's all. You all know that I have got quite a large sum of money in the building society and at times like this having money can be very useful. We are not going to be on the street, for goodness sake, and we have got three months to sort ourselves out."

Mary was, in reality, grabbing hold of the family reins. She was old enough and, by now, experienced enough in the ways of life to know that the responsibility for steering her family through this crisis lay firmly on her shoulders. "Tomorrow," she continued, "I intend to discuss our situation with Philip Manders. I have worked for him for over four years now and all the advice he has ever given me in the past has been sound, and worked out well for me. I will listen to him before we start jumping into anything and, in the meantime, I for one will not allow that Evans' girl to turn my life into a misery, and I will be disappointed with you lot if you let her do it to you, so get your chins up and let's move on."

"Don't forget, I've still got the house in the town," piped up Aunty Jo, "but somehow, the last thing I want to do is tip them out. They've been there for nearly twenty years and pay the rent as regular as clockwork. I've barely touched that rent so there is a tidy bit of cash I can put my hands on if necessary. It will all be yours one day, our Mary, so in the end it's really up to you what we do. I must say, I do agree that we must not let those Evans' tread all over us. I'll bet her mother has had something to do with this lot. I told you all those years ago that they weren't to be trusted, and now I've been proved right!"

Mary had her private discussion with Philip the following afternoon. She had mentioned to him that she needed a word rather urgently on a personal matter, when he arrived at nine o'clock.

"Will it keep until about half past two?" he asked. "I'm under pressure a bit this morning with one thing and another, but this afternoon doesn't look too bad."

"Yes, that will do fine," said Mary and at around 2.45 p.m. he beckoned her into his office. She thanked him for finding time for her and then proceeded to outline the previous evening's conversation with Elizabeth Evans.

"Well, well," he said, "fat lot of good that's going to do them, isn't it? They haven't been the most popular people in the parish for a few years, and now this will just about put the tin hat on it. It's not very often you can see an instant answer to things but what comes jumping straight out at me, Mary, is, if the cottage is going to be sold, go and buy the bloody thing! You can afford it. It's another asset in your portfolio and, hey-presto, problem solved."

"I can't," was Mary's reply. "I just can't live there anymore. Elizabeth Evans hates me with a real passion – I haven't got a clue why, not the foggiest idea, but I just know she does. It's in her looks and in her words, it's in the cut of her jib every time she sees me, and in the curl of her lips at the merest sight of me, as if she's trodden in some dog mess. I honestly can't wait to get out of the cottage. It's as though there is a river of venom and malice flooding down the farm drive into our front garden, and I simply want out as soon as possible."

"Phew, you are determined, aren't you?" Philip said. He was searching his mind to find the right advice to offer and realised that, above all, Mary needed someone to talk to, someone to share her troubles with. "Listen," he continued, "you have dropped this in my lap and certainly I will help you to sort things out, but I need a day or two to think about all your options. Just take comfort from the fact that I am here for you. Let's have another chat tomorrow afternoon when I've had time to sleep on it."

Mary went home and slept on it also. She slept fitfully, her mind turning over and over, awash with all the possibilities the future might hold for her and her family. She concerned herself that she had never revealed to Philip Manders the circumstances of Molly's will. She had asked him to help and advise her, but had not revealed to him the full extent of her prospects. She made a decision to tell him in the morning and reasoned that as he knew all the rest of her business affairs, it was now vital that he knew of Molly's bequest.

When she told Philip the facts of the inheritance she was looking forward to, he was somewhat taken aback. "My word, Mary, what a prospect, and what a lucky young lady you are. I will say, it couldn't happen to a nicer person but, my God, I don't know – two houses in the town, thousands in the building society, and the prospects of seventy acres of top grade land with a cottage and buildings dropping into your lap! You may be on the verge of eviction from Crest Farm but you are in a great position to come through that with all flags flying. You shouldn't have a worry in the world."

"Well, I do worry how I am going to manage it all and how I can do the best for everybody, and how and where we are all going to finish up," she replied.

"Yes, I do understand," responded Philip, "but look, what you have just told me could have a huge bearing on your present predicament. There are already several possibilities bouncing around in my head. Let me have the next couple of days and over the weekend to consider your options. I will speak to you again on Monday morning but believe you me young Mary, there are thousands of folk out there who would like to be in your boat, so stop worrying."

The weekend came and went. Mary had told her dad and Aunty Jo that Mr Philip was looking into things, that he would try to help them, and that she was going to talk to him again on Monday. She urged them not to become despondent and tried to cheer them up by saying that they should all look on it as a new beginning.

She saw Philip on Monday and he started his discourse with the words, "Mary, I am so excited for you. I made a couple of telephone calls earlier and the things I have unearthed are simply wonderful. The magic words are 'barn conversion'. Let's get planning permission to convert that big, old barn of Molly's into a house. I have confirmed that it ticks all the boxes with the planners, it's fifty yards away from her cottage, and the authorities are encouraging this type of development. There are two obstacles as far as I can see: where do you all live for the eight or nine months it will take to get the permission and build it, and Molly will have to agree to either sell or lease the barn to you. What do you think?"

Mary's brain was spinning. "Well, at face value it sounds marvellous," she began. "Dad and Grandad will still be in the country and able to potter about outside, and I would gladly move down there tomorrow. It would be wonderful to have a brand new kitchen and bathroom and so on, but there is one huge snag – what is Molly going to say to it all? At the moment it feels to me that we would be invading her privacy, barging in on her life. It seems as though I would be taking over before my time somehow."

"Well," responded Philip, "I believe that if Molly has so much respect and affection for you that she has bequeathed her entire estate to you, she will easily recognise the predicament you and your family are in, and readily agree to this way forward. Go and ask her, tell her it must all be done legally, and see what she says. It strikes me that the tidiest arrangement would be for you to have a ninety-nine year lease on the barn at a peppercorn rent of, say £1 per year. When Molly passes on you would inherit your own lease and at that point you could scrap it. That development will be highly valuable. It will appreciate in value as the years go by and it will be somewhere wonderful for you all to live, also you can keep your eye on Billy into the bargain. Go and ask her, Mary, and if she says 'no' we will have to think again."

Mary was not sure; she could see all the advantages of Philip's idea but was still concerned that the whole thing would put Molly's whole way of life into turmoil. As usual with Mary, she was considering other people's feelings and welfare before her own. "I will think about it for a few days. A week has already gone by since we had notice to quit, so I mustn't take too long. We'll talk again on Monday or Tuesday, and thank you for all your help, we are so grateful."

On the Friday and Saturday, she said nothing at home about Philip's plan. She kept racking her brain at all the consequences that might ensue if they followed his advice.

Would Molly be upset or worried in any way? Would she feel that she was being used? Or that Mary was trying to take advantage of her huge generosity? Mary's mind was not clear – she was muddled and indecisive.

On the Sunday afternoon she found herself walking gently up to the spinney at the top of Crest Farm. She visited it quite often, mostly for the glorious landscape, but also for the absolute solitude and silence it afforded her. The trunk of the fallen tree her mother had sat on eighteen years before was still there. It was her intention to settle herself down for half an hour or so and have a good think. As she rounded the spinney and approached the spot, she saw her – sat in the grass alongside the fallen tree, her knees pulled tightly up to her chin, her ample black cloak and dress concealing everything except that unforgettable face, the gypsy! Strangely, the icy quivers Mary had experienced before were not there.

"Hello, duckie," the gypsy began. "It's yer ode Granny Harris cum to see yer agen. Don't be werritin', I'se got nuthin' but good feelin's for yer and some more advice for yer as 'ull be to yer 'vantage."

"Who are you, and where do you live?" asked Mary.

"I'm Billy Perkins' granny, that's who I am and that's fer sure, everybody knows it. I 'elps me own as much as I can, that's wot I duz. I lives in the lanes an' bridleways, up in the hills and down by the river, under the hedgerows, under the stars and wherever me nose teks me. Now I'm here to tell yer what yer must do. You'm ponderin' 'bout gooin' to live at Molly's ent yer? Well doun't werrit no more."

"How do you know that?" whispered Mary.

"I just duz, I just duz," she replied and continued, "Molly will welcome yer with arms wide open her 'ull. End of 'er tether down ther' Molly is. It's all bin gettin' a bit too much for 'er lately. 'Er wants help, and if you guz to live ther', it'll be right tidy for 'er and 'er'll know it. Jus' aks 'er, 'er'll jump at it, that's all. I'll be on me way now."

"Listen," said Mary, "I have never had a chance to say thank you for the painting. I am so grateful, and when will I see you again? And where are you going now?"

"Doun't fuss yerself," came the reply, "I'm gooin' back where I cum from, and yer wunt never need to see me agen, duckie. It wunt be easy but you'm gonna be alright now." Her deeply wrinkled, mahogany face broke into the semblance of a toothless smile, and she rose and hobbled away down the hill.

"Thanks again," shouted Mary.

She flourished her walking stick without so much as a backward glance and followed the path for about a hundred yards to the stile in the hedgerow below. Mary watched as she climbed the stile and seemed to disappear into some huge hole on the other side. She had vanished, she was no more, although the evidence of her recent presence lingered once more in Mary's nostrils.

Mary's mind was made up – she would speak to Molly the following evening on her way home from work. She would normally have called anyway, to see Billy. 'What shall I say?' she thought. 'How shall I put it? How shall I begin?'

Throughout that Sunday evening and whilst she was at work on Monday, words and phrases were turning over and over in her mind. She found it difficult to concentrate on anything, her mind was elsewhere. She drove into Molly's yard at a quarter to six, with her heart in her mouth, feeling so nervous she could barely breathe. She tapped the door and walked in with her usual "It's only me," and Molly responded with her usual, "Come on in, there's a cup o' tea on the table."

"Can I have a word with you, Molly?" she began.

"Word, word about what?"

Mary then explained the circumstances of their looming eviction from the cottage, and how Elizabeth Evans had put things, and the predicament she and all her family were now in.

"Well, bugger me," said Molly, "who'd o' thought they could stoop so low. Things as a way of turnin' round on folk as duz things like that but, God alive, girl, what am you all goin' to do?"

Well, actually," replied Mary, "I wondered if we could come and live here?"

"Yes, yes, but wer in creation could I put yer all?" said Molly. "If I'd got room you'd be welcome but ther's only three rooms upstairs. Wer the devil would yer all goo?"

"Well, we could live in the barn over there," Mary nodded her head indicating the barn across the yard.

"Live in the barn like a lot of cattle? You'd all be dead uv newmonium or summat within a month or two."

"No, it's not like that, Molly," explained Mary. She proceeded to outline everything Philip Manders had put to her and what the barn could be like if it was developed. "But please, Molly, if you don't think it is a good idea, we'll think of something else. The last thing in the world I want to do is to upset you in any way. Please understand, there are other things we can do but it seemed so good, the thought of living down here with you and Billy."

"Mary, my love, if that's what you wants to do, you'm welcome. If that's what it'll tek to get you lot out of trouble, you'm more than welcome. It strikes me I might as well give yer the barn now, arter all, it's gooin' to be yorn one day any road." Molly continued, "I 'as bin a'strugglin' a bit lately, I don't mind tellin' yer. This market gardenin' malarkie's a'catchin' up on me a bit, so if yer dad wants to lend a hand, that's great. I 'spect I shall 'at to pack it all up one day 'afore it packs me up, but yes, yes, yes, tell Philip Manders to get it all drawn up and get on wiv it."

Mary was overjoyed. "Don't talk about packing up, Molly, you have got years left in you yet. What you need to do is slow down a bit and, once we get down here, I have got loads of ideas that will improve things for you."

Molly reached across and placed a big, fat, weathered hand on Mary's arm. "When you walked in here half an hour ago, I 'ad not an idea in the world as to what you 'ad to say, but now I'se real pleased, really happy about it all Mary, so just get on wiv it as quickly as yer can." As they stood up, they hugged each other for a little while. "Don't matter what I duz for you Mary, it will never repay what you's dun fer Billy." Molly wiped a stray tear that was rolling down her cheek as she said it.

Mary hurried home and immediately broke the news to everyone. She was, by now, so enthusiastic about the project she could barely get her words out quickly enough. "Just think," she said, "lovely new bathroom and toilet, new kitchen and laundry, cosy wood burning stoves, and all exactly where we want to be, and where we want to stay for that matter." She continued, barely stopping to breathe, "And I know what we'll do in the meantime. I'll buy a big caravan, put it in the yard down there, all connected to the drains and everything. I am sure we'll manage just for a few months while the barn is being done, then when we move in the caravan can be sold. If I lose a bit it doesn't matter when you look at the bigger picture."

"How much is it all going to cost?" asked Aunty Jo.

"Well, Philip thought that to do the job nicely and finish it all to a good standard, about two thousand five hundred pounds, but look, I've got over six thousand pounds in the building society now so it's not a problem, and it's all so perfect, for all of us. Let's face it, when Molly's time comes and the place is mine, none of us would want to live in her old cottage, would we? Please say you like the idea and that we can all stay together."

"Mary, I've known you for too long not to know when your mind's made up," replied Aunty Jo. "Doesn't matter what we say, you've got the bit between your teeth and you're going to do it. Anyway, sounds alright to me, although I'm not sure about the caravan bit. We shall have to see, but I expect we'll cope."

"What about you, Dad?"

"Whatever you wants, Mary," he responded, "least I'll be able to knock about outside and do a bit round the farm for Molly. I'm not going back up that drive again, that's for sure, not after this lot!"

The following day, Tuesday, was market day and everyone at Barker's was busy. Although Mary did sort of whisper to Philip that she knew what she was going to do, there was no time to expand. "I'll tell you tomorrow," she said.

On the Wednesday, Philip called her into his office and said, "Well, what's the decision?"

"We all think the barn conversion is a brilliant idea," said Mary. "I've asked Molly and she loves it, can't wait to get us there, that's it really." She told him about the caravan idea.

"Good thinking," he replied, "you will be able to keep your eye on everything as it's going on, I like that. We had better get things started then, no time to lose, but you'll all need a bit of patience."

During the following days, Philip introduced Mary to a local architect, Brian Clegg, who would prepare plans and submit them to the district council. At the same time, the plans would go out to a few builders who specialised in renovations, asking for quotations. Brian Clegg paid several visits to the cottage with possibilities and ideas for the property, discussing them with Mary and her family, and making sure that his drawings fulfilled their needs and expectations. He arranged for a concrete slab to be laid to receive the caravan and for its connection to the drains.

"You'll be able to use that slab for a shed one day," he remarked.

They all liked Brian and appreciated the work he was doing for them. Eight weeks after receiving their eviction notice, Mary and her family all moved down the hill to the caravan in Molly's yard. As they left the cottage for the last time, their moods were different. Mary and Aunty Jo were sat in their cars waiting impatiently for Dick and Grandad to join them for the short journey down to Molly's. Dick and Grandad, however, lingered for a while. Grandad looked across the fields from the kitchen window. He had visions of his beloved Rose, and his heart was choking with emotion at leaving the place that had been his heaven, had been everything he had ever wanted out of life. Dick was in a similar state of mind. This had been his home with Joan – a place that was the source of so much happiness but, alas, the place of so much heartache.

"Come on, Jack," he said, "it's time to move on."

Up at the farm, Elizabeth Evans was heard to remark that "everyone finds their own level eventually, and now they are in a caravan, finally they've found theirs". She sang a different tune a few months later as the barn took shape and she realised what was happening.

After a few days, Grandad moved out of the caravan into the spare room in Molly's cottage – he couldn't get used to living in a house on wheels!

Aunty Jo loved it. "Do you know, I have always turned my nose up at caravans and caravan holidays, but you couldn't want anything much better than this. Everything is all so convenient and handy."

Philip Manders had allowed them to store some items of furniture in a spare building down in the market, and with the builders appointed, specialists in renovations, things took off.

As the months rolled by, the old barn was transformed – stripped down to its bare sandstone walls and beams, relined, reroofed, and fitted out to produce an extensive, modern home, full of character, old-world charm and cosiness. They all loved it, and seven months after moving into the caravan, they relocated into the barn. Life was good again!

CHAPTER ELEVEN

The next two years saw Mary making many changes at Molly's place. Firstly, she changed the name from Half Crest Farm to Crest Pool. She thought it sounded better. "Not so much of a mouthful," she said. Gradually Molly did wind down and took it easier. Dick helped her as much as he could, but Dick was no market gardener.

"Seems to me like loads of back sloggin' hard work to produce two penn'orth of nothin'," he said.

Mary gradually changed the farming policy of the little place. She reduced and contained the market gardening to about seven acres, and five acres of that was for potatoes. The rest was for a few strawberries and raspberries which Billy looked after, and which were marketed by way of 'pick your own'. The public were invited to do just that, and they did, in their droves. Molly weighed their pickings and took their money with glee. "Beats hard work this duz," she declared.

The other land was seeded down – grass, Mary reasoned, was the easiest thing to grow in England. In the summer months about seventy or so strong steers grazed the upper meadows, and were sold off at the rate of about ten per week through September and October. The land would be rested through the winter months and then the following April the process would be repeated again.

Mary's next innovation was the opening of a farm shop. She persuaded Molly to let her develop one of the smaller barns nearer the road. It needed reroofing and new windows, but for quite a modest sum it created space to lay out vegetables, eggs, pickles, jams, cakes, and many other commodities, all local produce and some home grown. From a modest beginning, when it was only open on Fridays and Saturdays, it flourished and was soon open seven days a week. Whilst many of the goods on offer were produced on the farm – the eggs and potatoes, for example – much had to be bought in. This was a job for Dick and Billy. Every Tuesday and Friday Dick, now driving again, would visit the wholesale market in Chesterton in Molly's old van and bring back a full range of fruit and vegetables. With Molly manning the place, it thrived. She was remembered from the market and many of her old clients came up to shop and to enjoy her humorous banter. "Would yer like a few of my nice home grown bananas?" was one of her cracks. "Grown right here on Crest Hill," she would chortle. With the shop soon taking a thousand pounds a week, she took on a bit of help at the weekends, an old friend, Doris Field, who lived down in the town.

"My God," Molly declared, "beats standin' in the old market, this duz, freezin' yer tits off all winter and sweatin' um off all summer!"

They had to get planning permission and change of usage in order to open the shop. There was one objection, from Elizabeth Evans at Crest Farm. She contended that the increased traffic on the lane would be a danger, particularly to horses and riders who had used the highway for decades. Her objection was ignored, but the granting of permission further irritated and inflamed the malice she held for Mary.

Mary shrugged her shoulders. "Whatever problems she has are her problems," she said. "I'm not going to wage any sort of feud with her. I just refuse to be drawn into that sort of thing. We'll just carry on working hard and doing our best. As far as I am concerned, she can wallow in her own spite and envy – I'm not joining in."

"She'll choke on her own bile one of these days," said Aunty Jo.

Mary, as usual, had sought the advice of Philip Manders about the planning permission for the shop.

"Let's see, you have been living there for over two years now so it should not be a problem. You will have to prove you are selling at least some things that are home grown, or home produced, and then everything should be quite straightforward. Leave it to me, Mary, I'll deal with it for you, but before you leave there is something I want to tell you. I want you to know, before the inevitable gossip reaches your ears, that Hilary and I are separating. The girls are both now in their late teens. Sophie is already at University and Grace is going next year. They both know what is happening and so far things seem fine, a bit upset but basically OK. There's no-one else, we've just grown apart. Hilary is a Londoner you know and has never really settled out in the sticks, so she is going back there to be near her mother. We own a flat and she's taking that over. Anyway, I felt that after working so closely together for the last seven years, I ought to let you know what is happening, before the tongues start wagging."

"Thank you," murmured Mary, "my tongue won't wag, I do assure you."

They went about their daily business and no more was said. Tongues did start to wag. Aunty Jo was the first to mention it. "What's this I hear about your boss leaving his wife?" she asked.

"I have heard," replied Mary, "but it's none of my business, nor anyone else's as far as I can tell." They left it at that.

The business plan Mary had put into place at Molly's was now working perfectly. The shop was thriving, the pick-your-own, though seasonal, took care of itself. There were a nice few potatoes to dig every autumn, to be sold in the shop, and the grazing cattle were bringing in healthy profits. Apart from employing a contractor to lift the potatoes and Doris Field to help in the shop, they did all the work themselves. It was all self-contained and profitable.

Billy simply loved having Mary and her family so close. He would do literally anything to help them, from chopping logs for the woodburners to cleaning Mary's and Aunty Jo's cars. Under Molly's supervision, he took care of the raspberries and strawberries, he helped Dick with the cattle and poultry, went to market with him, and did most of the general cleaning and tidying round the shop and around the yard. Mary liked everything spick and span, shipshape and polished. It usually was, and she would often say, "everything looks lovely, Bill. Well done, well done".

Billy was as happy as the proverbial lark, and although Grandad was becoming increasingly immobile and forgetful, everything about the place felt good and comfortable. They were a good team and as the years rolled by, they prospered.

It wasn't at all like that at Crest Farm, in fact, quite the reverse. Harry Evans had passed away the year before. In his eighty third year, he was a broken man, with a broken heart. Dick and Jack attended his funeral – Jack on two sticks, and with great difficulty. They paid their respects but were not acknowledged by the family.

"Over eighty years up there between us," Dick said, "and you would have thought we were strangers."

Elizabeth and Michael Mason had started gambling, backing horses on a daily basis. In spite of their supposed 'inside knowledge', generally speaking they lost, and whilst stupidly chasing their losses, lost more and more. Two years after selling the farm cottage, they were again under pressure from the bank to clear their debts. This time, after much thought, they decided to sell the vast majority of the lower land, valuable waterside meadows amounting to nearly two hundred acres. They would keep ten acres around the house and stables, enough to gallop the horses when necessary, and the four hundred acres of poor, upper land, mostly moor and heath, but the prime, rich lower land was to be sold, in reality ruining the farm's future prospects. As a neighbouring farmer remarked in the market one morning, "That's fucked that place up for good and all. They must be mental. They'd be better off selling the lot and let somebody else run it properly, the way it always was."

Elizabeth gave instructions to an estate agent in Chesterton which meant that Barker's did not handle the sale of the water meadows. They did, however, receive copies of the particulars of the land and its imminent sale. Mary saw these particulars and was ready to pounce. As always, her next stop was Philip Manders and she explained her plans. As always, her basic philosophy was growing grass. It was relatively easy, she contended. She had cut her teeth at beef farming in the last two years but was now restricted by lack of acreage and buildings. She knew that there were some amazing Ministry grants available for the construction of new farm buildings, up to seventy-five percent of the total cost in some cases. Given more acreage and suitable buildings, she calculated that she could turn up to three hundred cattle a year off the two hundred and fifty acres, all fed on home grown grass and cereals.

Philip listened patiently to her for some fifteen minutes then he broke his silence. "Mary," he began, "you are doing so well, making such a success of that little place up there, and you are all so happy. The last thing in the world I want is to see you overstretch yourself and get into trouble. You will get summers of drought when the grass won't grow, you will need to take on more help with all the problems that can bring and, furthermore, I will warn you, that land will be so much sought after. I can name at least four local farmers who are already sniffing round to buy it. It's going to make a lot of money, probably as much as twenty-five thousand pounds – enough to buy five houses."

Philip continued, pointing out to Mary that at the moment the only thing she owned at Crest Pool was the barn – Molly still owned all the rest. "What about if she changes her will at some stage?" he asked. "I'm sorry to be such a wet blanket, such a merchant of doom and gloom, but you must give all these things careful consideration. I suggest that in the first place you should discuss all these things with Molly, tell her what your plans are and see what she comes up with. Perhaps some sort of partnership between you and Molly might be appropriate. She could then leave you her share in the joint venture. I don't know for sure – that's just one idea – but I do know that her owning this bit and you owning that bit is all a bit messy. It's just not tidy and I am uncomfortable with it. As a matter of interest, how much ready cash have you got at your disposal for the purchase of this land and the construction of a farm building?"

"About twenty five thousand pounds, I think. Don't forget the work on the barn cost nearly three thousand," Mary replied. Philip's eyes opened wide with surprise. "We have earned over fifteen thousand pounds clear profit in the last four years, and it's all in my building society account.

It's been building up nicely now for over six years with the interest and rent from the houses, and the profit from the shop and everything. Dad and Billy get a few pounds every week and seem very happy with their lot, and Molly just says she doesn't need anything – got plenty in the bank to live off, she says. She has a few things out of the shop, of course. My calculations tell me that for the land, building, extra implements and extra cattle, I will need probably thirty-five thousand pounds to be comfortable. I thought I might possibly sell the houses to make up the shortfall."

"That is a possibility," he replied, "but go and talk to Molly first, and we'll take it from there."

Mary did talk to Molly that very night. She explained the opportunity that had presented itself – two hundred acres of prime land, right next door, adjoining their own, was up for sale. She explained her idea for a large herd of beef cattle with a building for overwintering.

Molly knew all about silage. "Well, what's stopping yer?" she declared.

"Mr Philip thinks you and I should do it in partnership," she replied. "He thinks that the entire holding, your cottage and land, our barn with the new land and buildings, should all be together on one set of deeds."

"Let me just say this," said Molly, "it's bin on me mind for a little while, what with all the improvements and everything you've dun here. As long as me and Billy can live in this house fer the rest of our natural, I'se willin' to turn the lot over into yer name now, next wik if yer like. I'm gooin' to be seventy in a couple of years, for Christ's sake, and I ent gooin' into no new partnerships with anybody. All I wants is to see the rest of me days out, comfortable like, up here on this hill, and fer our Billy to have some sort of future. Get in touch with Mr Wilkes. Tell 'im to get it all drawn up so I can stay 'ere like I said, an' I'll turn it all over to you now. You'm gooin' to 'ave it one day any road up, so if it's tidier to do it now, let's do it. My God, Girl, you'm tekkin' summat on, I'll be buggered if you aint. You'll want a lot of help an' a deal o' luck an 'all."

"That's just great, Molly, I'll tell Mr Philip tomorrow what you've said and we'll take it from there. In the meantime, mum's the word, not a word to a single soul, not a word. And, by the way, thanks a million."

Mary lost no time in breaking the news to Philip of Molly's willingness to comply with any arrangement that would facilitate the purchase of the land.

"Right," he said, "I know how determined you are so let's get on with it. I have listened to your plans for the beef unit and so on. I don't profess to be any sort of farmer but, from what I've seen, looking at the farming world from the outside, everything you have described does make sound common sense." Philip continued to explain that the land was going to be auctioned to the highest bidder on 26th June at The White Hart Hotel in Chesterton. "Now whatever you do, don't go near that land in the next month, don't give anyone an inkling that you are interested, and you certainly should not attend the auction personally. I will go and bid on your behalf. No-one will have a clue who I am acting for. If Elizabeth Evans gets the slightest whiff that you are in for it, you know she will do her best to make sure you don't get it."

Philip continued, "I have also been giving some thought to your finances and taken some advice. I would urge you not to sell those houses. Keep them – you'll never regret it. It looks to me as though you need to raise about ten thousand pounds." He explained that there was an institution known as the Agricultural Mortgage Corporation, run by the Ministry of Agriculture. They specialised in providing loans specifically for the purchase of land and would loan up to seventy-five per cent of the purchase price.

"Now that you are going to own a further seventy acres," Philip said, "plus these two hundred, together with all your other assets, and the excellent performance of your business, particularly the shop, it will be a doddle, an absolute walk in the park to borrow ten thousand off the AMC. I could arrange it on the 'phone in a matter of minutes. It will all have to go through your solicitor, of course, but there you are, if you still want the land, you can have it." He paused for breath. "One thing crosses my mind, Mary, does this mean that Barker's will be losing you? You've been my right hand these last few years, you know."

"I'm not sure," she replied. "I need to think about it, but not straight away I wouldn't think. I may ask you to cut my hours down a bit, or just work two or three days a week perhaps, but whatever, I won't let you down and you will get loads of notice."

"Right," said Philip. "Number one, get Molly's land signed over a.s.a.p., number two, keep your lips sealed and, number three, keep your fingers crossed. Personally, I don't think there will be anyone in that auction room with a stronger hand than you so, good luck!"

The next few weeks soon rolled by. The night of the auction came and Mary waited patiently at home by the telephone. As Philip had predicted, the room at the White Hart was packed with prospective purchasers but the sale was short and sharp. Having described all the merits of the land, the auctioneer inquired if anyone was willing to open the bidding at thirty thousand. There was deathly silence.

"Come on, then," he said, "twenty-five then, and let's get on with it." Philip's hand shot up. "I've got a bid of twenty-five thousand pounds, is there any advance?"

"That's sorted ninety per cent of them out," thought Philip as a murmur spread around the room.

"Two hundred and fifty," came a voice from the back.

"Twenty-five thousand two hundred and fifty," declared the auctioneer. He also realised that Philip's bid had blown most of the potential buyers out of the water.

"Five hundred," piped up Philip.

In spite of the auctioneer's pleas, there were no more bids. "Sold to Mr Philip Manders, on behalf of a client I imagine, Philip."

"Correct," came the reply. Philip duly handed over a cheque for two thousand five hundred and fifty pounds as a ten per cent deposit. Settlement would be in seven days' time, and solicitors would then exchange contracts. No-one, least of all Elizabeth Evans, had any idea that the mystery client was Mary Jones. It was fairly general knowledge around the farming circle that Mary was doing quite well, but no-one in their wildest dreams would have bracketed her in the company that could afford this land. When the news broke, the shock amongst the local yeomen and around the markets and taverns was seismic.

'How the bloody hell 'as her got herself into a position to be able to afford that sort of money?' was a typical comment. Some of them were full of admiration for her, some of them a bit cynical, sceptical, and jealous. Elizabeth Evans was apoplectic. When she heard who had bought her land, she was at first disbelieving. As it dawned on her that it was indeed true, she shook with rage and fury. Her face changed, firstly to chalk white, and almost immediately to bright red. She telephoned her solicitor to inquire if the transaction of the land was irretrievable.

"Certainly is," he declared. "I have exchanged contracts with the purchaser. Furthermore, if you sell anything at auction, title to the item passes to the last bidder the instant the hammer falls. There can be no backing out by either party once that hammer drops."

She slammed the 'phone back into place. "I'll poison that land before she takes it over," she spat. "I'll fucking poison it!"

Everyone who had daily contact with Elizabeth kept their distance for the next few days. She went round tongue-lashing anyone and everyone on the slightest pretext. Her mother, during one of her visits, declared that she could not understand what Elizabeth's problem was.

"Why do you hate that girl so much?" she asked. "I remember she helped you once, when you fell off your pony in the orchard, and you thought she was quite nice then."

"You don't know half," retorted Elizabeth. "She used to come creeping round up here, sneaking and spying on us. You didn't know that did you? And what about her constantly cothering up to that thick ginger kid from down the lane, that Billy whatever his name is? Is that perverse or what? Some women get a kick from having sexual activity with disabled and retarded men. He's in that bracket, you know. He looks to me as though he'd be more at home in a zoo, and nothing would surprise me where she is concerned."

"Lizzie, that's outrageous and you know it is. You've got your money, you've cleared the bank off, just get on with enjoying life, that's my advice," her mother replied. "She's more than likely bitten off more than she can chew anyway, so let her get on with it," she concluded.

The next few months were just so busy for Mary. She had taken the land over in September – too late to do much with it immediately – and got on with things like planning permission for the building and the securing of a Ministry grant to help pay for it. There were dozens of forms to fill in and so much information to provide but she got there in the end. Philip had introduced Mary to a firm of accountants in the town, James Parker and Partners. With the help of Alec Foster, one of the partners, she formulated a business plan and a business account was opened with the bank. Previously Mary's personal account had accommodated all the business transactions. Having purchased the land with her own money, plus the ten thousand pound mortgage from the AMC, it left her with around eight thousand pounds to provide money for the barn, extra implements and livestock – cattle to graze the fields – but she was short. One hundred and twenty cattle were needed at a cost of around two hundred and fifty pounds each or, in total, thirty thousand pounds.

Alec Foster introduced her to the manager of a local bank, an appointment was made and Philip Manders went with her to see the manager, John Robertson. The position was explained to him and the need for some working capital during the summer months.

"Let me get this straight," he said, "you are twenty-seven years old, you own two hundred and seventy acres of land, two houses, a barn development and a farm shop, plus a farm cottage which is occupied on a none rental basis, and your only liability is a ten thousand pound mortgage with the AMC."

"That's about right," said Philip.

"How the dickens have you accumulated all that at your tender age?" queried the bank manager.

"It's a long story," said Mary, "but I have been very, very lucky to say the least, plus I have been well advised," and she nodded towards Philip.

"Well, Miss Jones, I will have absolutely no problem in setting up a twenty-five thousand pound overdraft facility for you to help you buy a hundred cattle for your fields. You can draw down on it from March 1st next year, and we will expect it cleared by October 30th. I will need you to sign a debenture in relation to that stock so that basically, the cattle are ours until you sell them. This is all perfectly normal bank procedure." Philip nodded. The bank manager concluded, "Well, whatever your story is, Miss Jones, it must be quite a remarkable one, and I do wish you all the luck in the world."

The following spring saw a hundred or more fine steers grazing the riverside meadows at Crest Pool Farm. Mary knew, from her experience in the market, those cattle dealers she could trust. One particularly, Tom Bailey, had an impeccable reputation for honesty and fair dealing but they weren't all like that. Tom, for a modest commission, bought and transported the cattle in lots of about twenty. As Mary's own buildings and handling facilities were not quite ready, he took them back to his own farm and wormed and drenched them all before turning them out at Mary's. Thirty acres of spring barley was sown on Molly's old land, with the remaining forty acres set aside for silage making as soon as the new buildings were complete – sometime in early June. Mary had calculated that the sale of the grazing steers in September and October would both pay off the overdraft, and leave sufficient surplus to buy young stock to overwinter in the new barn. These would be fed on the silage and barley to come off Molly's old land, and would mean she would not have to buy cattle for grazing the following spring.

More help was needed. It went on alright for a few months with some casual weekend labour pulled in, and the use of contractors to cut grass for silage, and combine the barley. Mary knew, however, in the longer term, it wasn't the answer, so she headhunted a man by the name of Tom White who was the son of a man who had worked for Harry Evans at Crest Farm. He was about Mary's age and knew the farming world inside out. Employed at the moment as a lorry driver for a firm of cattle hauliers, Mary thought he was wasted as he could turn his hand to anything on the farm from tractor driving to sheep shearing, from cattle husbandry to poultry keeping. Mary craftily asked him to call to discuss the transportation of some cattle to the abattoir.

"By the way," she said, as they concluded their discussions, "I'm looking for a top man up here now, sort of joint farm manager with Dad. It will be a well-paid job, so if you hear of anyone looking for that sort of position who has the right experience, let me know."

"You never know," he replied, "it might suit me, but I'm not sure you'd think I was up to it."

"Look," said Mary, "go home and have a chat with your wife, and if you think you might be interested, telephone me and come up, the pair of you, and we'll have a talk about it over a cup of tea."

He did telephone; he and his wife did visit, and Mary appointed him with immediate effect. Mary's judgement was good. As the years rolled by, Tom proved to be a real diamond and a huge influence on the development of Crest Pool into a highly efficient, highly profitable beef farm. Apart from the eggs and potatoes for the farm shop, they concentrated on, and specialised in, the production of high quality beef. Their system was self-contained. Other than mineral salts and fish meal to add to the barley, they bought nothing in. Their stock was keenly sought after by the local abattoirs and they thrived.

Billy, also, was thriving – thriving on the newfound variety in the tasks he was asked to perform, in the new company he now had, and in the general feeling of enterprise and success that flowed from every corner of the place. He often went across to the barn for his evening meal. Mary had bought him a couple of track suits and put in place a strict routine which he was required to stick to.

"When you finish work, straight into the bath," she said, "put a clean track suit on and then you can come over to eat. In the morning, get back into your working shirt and overalls. I don't mind you coming over to the barn, every day if you like, but you're not coming over smelling like a polecat."

Billy hung on her every word and followed her instructions to the letter.

Sadly, Grandad passed away that winter, in his ninetieth year. It was as though he had decided his time had come, and for the last two weeks of his life he never left his chair, refusing even to go to bed. On her return from work at half past five, Aunty Jo had put a cup of tea on his little table.

"There's your tea, Jack," she said, and he raised his hand in acknowledgement. She went back half an hour later – the tea was untouched, Jack had gone quietly to sleep and would not wake up. Mary was his only blood relative which meant his funeral was very quiet and personal. He was laid beside his beloved Rose in St Mark's churchyard, and was remembered with great affection by everyone who had ever known him.

CHAPTER TWELVE

A year passed by. Things continued to develop but not without the odd crisis. One day someone spitefully opened the gates to some of the fields at the bottom of the lane, releasing the cattle out on to the road. After a big hue and cry, they were all rounded up and returned to the safety of their pastures. Chains and padlocks were quickly fitted to all the gates and, after several worrying hours, things returned to normal.

Jane White, Tom's wife, joined the team to help with the shop – in effect, she came to manage it. Jane was a happy-go-lucky type of character, always positive, always smiling and bubbly. She would never let slip an opportunity to expose the humorous side of any situation. The customers loved her, and Molly quickly took her to her heart.

An awning was put into place across the full length of the rear wall and Jane, who was a keen gardener, introduced a range of hardy pot plants and shrubs. She brought in a range of freshly baked bread, delivered in daily from a local bakery. She also stocked greeting cards, cookery and gardening books, chinaware, and ornamental brasses. She had plans to put a small extension on to the building and open a tea and coffee shop. These plans were discussed with Mary who, sensibly, urged a little caution, a little patience. Not too much too soon was her message. "Let's see if the shop kicks on in the next six months, get Christmas behind us and then, all things being well, we will do it."

After discussions with Philip, Mary had reduced her hours at Barker's. A plan had been devised to phase the reduction in over a six month span. Mary now only worked four days, Monday to Thursday, and only from nine o'clock to 1 o'clock, sixteen hours per week.

"I would rather have you for sixteen hours than not at all," Philip declared.

A bright sixteen-year-old girl, fresh from school, had joined the office and, under Mary's supervision, things continued to run smoothly.

Philip took a great interest in, and kept a close eye on, Mary's progress at Crest Pool. Now living on his own, Mary had invited him to join them all for Sunday lunch. After Aunty Jo's roast beef and apple pie, they walked the farm viewing the growing crops and the grazing cattle. As they returned to the barn Philip said, "There are three main reasons for your success here, you know. Number one, you have a business plan and you have stuck to it. You concentrate solely on what you are good at and refuse to deviate from that area. Sheep farmers have been earning a nice few bob lately, as you well know, but you have not been tempted to get involved. You have stuck with your beef cattle. Number two is that farm shop – stroke of genius that was. It's the talk of the county, you know, and the weekly cash flow it gives you is priceless. Number three is easy – you are not up to your ears in debt to the bank, nor paying any crippling rents to landlords. It's an incredible thought but all this can be traced back to nine years ago, that bloody antique shop in Chesterton and that painting. It's amazing, quite amazing!"

"Don't forget Molly's contribution," Mary chipped in, "she's been amazing as well, and your advice and guidance has been, well, just invaluable."

"I wonder where it's all going to end," Philip said. "Just keep following your instincts and backing your judgement – that's my advice."

The dreadful news of Elizabeth Evans' suicide rocked the county. Michael Mason had found her hanging on a leather rein from a beam in the main stable block at 8 o'clock in the morning. There had been concerns about her mental health for some months – her notorious mood swings, one minute all sweetness and light, to be followed by displays of animated temper when she would spit her venom at anyone who crossed her path. Her mother was devastated. She had known for some time that the horse business was once more in a state of financial flux, and that Elizabeth now had little room to manoeuvre. She also knew that Elizabeth's mind had never properly recovered from the sale of the land to Mary Jones, something Elizabeth had seen as nothing short of abject humiliation.

Nancy and Gerald de Beau moved into Crest Farm but Nancy took great pains to let everyone know that it was only a temporary arrangement until things were tidied up.

"I just could not live here again," she said. "It's heartbreak hill for me, this place."

As Elizabeth's next of kin, she automatically inherited Crest Farm, or what was left of it, and she determined to get rid of it as fast as she possibly could. There was much sympathy from the entire farming community across the Ampleford area. Typically, country people put aside personal feelings, even for someone of such dubious popularity as Elizabeth. The death by suicide of a young woman, only just past thirty, was a tragedy, and they turned out in their droves for her funeral. Dick attended, but Mary contented herself with a letter of condolence to Nancy from everyone at Crest Pool. Aunty Jo didn't want to talk about it. "She didn't do us any favours, that's for sure," was her only remark.

Shortly after this tragic event, Philip asked Mary if he could return the Sunday lunch treat.

"You come to my house this time," he said. "Sophie and Grace are here for the weekend and you have never met them, I'm sure you will get on well."

There was one snag – Mary was going to have to do the cooking, a chore usually left to Aunty Jo, so she protested.

"Talk about putting me on the spot," she said, "what sort of impression will I leave on your girls if their lunch is rubbish?" They compromised – Philip booked them all in to the Green Dragon in Chesterton where the lunch was fabulous and Philip had been so right, Mary did get on with Sophie and Grace, like the proverbial house on fire. They all went back to Crest Pool for a cup of tea which gave Mary chance to show them round the farm and the shop. They were flabbergasted and full of admiration at her achievements.

Two weeks later, Philip extended another invitation to Mary. Barker's were deep into negotiations about a possible merger with a very large firm of estate agents based in London and he was required to attend a meeting there in two weeks' time. Mary had seen correspondence about the proposed merger and details of Philip's meeting, and had remarked, "Lucky you, I'd love to go to London one day and take Aunty Jo and Billy. They'd have their eyes opened for sure and I expect I would, too, for that matter."

The following day, Philip beckoned her into his office and said, "I've been thinking, now don't take this the wrong way but why don't you come to London with me? Please believe me, I have absolutely no ulterior motive – separate rooms and everything, I promise. Unfortunately I can't accommodate Aunty Jo and Billy, but if you want to come, you are welcome. My meeting is on the Friday afternoon, 2 o'clock to 5 o'clock, so we could stay for a couple of nights, do a musical, I'll show you the sights and we'll come back on Sunday. I don't pretend to be a Londoner but I do know it quite well so what do you think? It will all be on the firm's expenses and no questions asked."

Mary hesitated for a few seconds. 'My God,' she thought, 'I'm twenty-nine years old, why not?' "Yes," she said, "I would love to come, thank you for asking me."

Mary couldn't wait to get home to tell Aunty Jo and her dad. "Guess what, Aunty?" she commenced, "I'm going to London with Philip for three days in two weeks' time and will see Buckingham Palace and the Houses of Parliament. I'm so excited and looking forward to it so much." She watched Aunty Jo's face change – there was a distinct expression of disapproval written all over it.

"Hmph," she replied, "I didn't bring you up, our Mary, to go gallivanting off to London for weekends with married men."

"Oh, for God's sake, Aunty Jo," came the reply, "I've worked with Philip for twelve years now and trust him completely. Furthermore he's divorced and a perfect gentleman, and anyway, I'm twenty-nine, old enough to make my own mind up, and I'm going and that's it, so don't be so old fashioned."

"Call me old fashioned if you like but I know right from wrong and I hope you know what you are doing, that's all, I'll say no more!" Aunty Jo shut up and didn't mention the affair again.

The days fled by and Mary and Philip were soon boarding the 7.50 from Chesterton to London. Mary was fascinated by the journey as the high speed intercity express simply whizzed through the countryside. Looking out of the window she saw herds of cattle, horses, factory estates, canals, rivers, and rows of houses all flashing by in the blink of an eyelid – now they were there, now they were gone, split second images, no chance to study the things that might have been of interest, no chance to admire them or otherwise.

"It's so tantalising," she said to Philip. "I would love to get off and have a look at some of these places."

"At a hundred miles an hour I wouldn't advise it," he said.

The train was on time, arriving at Euston at 10.20, and they were soon travelling by taxi to their hotel in Russell Square. By the time they had sorted out their rooms and had a coffee and a sandwich at the hotel bar, it was time for Philip to set sail to the offices of Halcyon Estates for his meeting.

"I'll tell you what," said Philip, "to save you moping about all afternoon, jump into my taxi and we'll drop you off at Harrods. You can have a good nose round and, believe me, three hours in Harrods is nothing – you would need three days to see everything. I'll meet you in the Harrods' coffee bar as soon as I can, probably about 5.30ish."

"I'm in your hands," Mary replied.

Mary was completely blown away by London. She was wide-eyed at the huge, high buildings, at the cars, the taxis, the big red buses, their horns tooting and blaring, their engines roaring and the occasional squeal of their brakes; the pavements with hoards of people hurrying and scurrying and disappearing like columns of ants into the tube stations; city gents with their bowler hats, barrow boys wearing flat caps, elegant ladies in high fashion rig-outs; a busker with his harmonica and, occasionally, the rough sleeper with his mattress in a doorway. It was all so different to the bird song, the whisper of the breeze, and the gentle lowing of the cattle up on Crest Hill.

"Phew," she turned to Philip, "it's a bit different to Ampleford isn't it? Does it ever stop?"

He laughed, "You'll be glad to go home on Sunday, I'll wager. I get the impression you wouldn't like to live down here then?"

"No, I don't think so but it's so amazing. I thought there would be lots of hustle and bustle but nothing like this. It's so relentless."

Mary had a wonderful afternoon in Harrods, browsing as she had never browsed before. It was early September and by now the Christmas grotto was in full swing. She marvelled at the sheer size and scope of it all, the endless range of goods on display, floor after floor, an Aladdin's cave of merchandise of the very highest quality. Mary splashed out on a new pair of slippers for Aunty Jo, a waistcoat for her dad, and a snazzy pair of jeans for Billy. Her last purchase was a lovely pen and pencil set made in rolled gold, and presented in a small carved, silk-lined box. That was for Philip, a gesture of her appreciation for the marvellous time she was having. Philip met her as arranged and they taxied back to their hotel. They dined at a little Italian trattoria only a few yards from the hotel and, at last, Mary caught her breath, relaxed and tried to relive the last twelve hours. "Probably the most exciting time of my life," she told Philip.

"You wait till tomorrow," he said, "you ain't seen nothin' yet!"

On Saturday morning they jumped onto an open top bus for a sightseeing tour of the famous landmarks: Big Ben, Tower Bridge, St Paul's, Buckingham Palace, Marble Arch, Nelson's Column, and many more. They jumped off on the Chelsea Embankment, gazed across the river at the famous power station, had lunch in Pimlico, and caught the tube back to Soho. After a trip to Covent Garden where they watched the artistes, jugglers, buskers, and so on, they grabbed a pie and a pint, and taxied into the West End to the Coliseum to see *Kiss Me Kate*.

"There is nothing in the world quite like a West End musical," declared Philip. He was right – it was magical and Mary was spellbound.

By now, Mary was totally exhausted. "I'm having such a job to take it all in," she said, "I don't want to forget anything, not a single thing, but there's so much to absorb."

"Don't worry," replied Philip, "you never know, we might come back again next year."

"Is that a promise?" asked Mary.

"No, but you never know," was the answer.

On Sunday, they were due to return home at 4 o'clock, so they contented themselves with a quiet walk and strolled down the Bayswater Road admiring the works of the painters, sculptures and potters that were displayed along the pavement and hung from the park railings. They moved into Hyde Park and sat beside the Serpentine, reflecting on their last forty-eight memorable hours. They had lunch at the 'Inn on the Park' and, sitting beneath the trees in the warm sunshine, they declared their love for each other.

In truth, the mutual attraction and affection they held for each other went all the way back to their first meeting in the market, nearly thirteen years ago. Twelve years of working so closely together meant that for professional reasons, their feelings had to be subdued and stifled – now they were liberated and free.

For Mary's part, the fact was that her admiration for Philip had meant that all the numerous suitors who had sought her attention over the years had been compared to her boss – he had been her benchmark and in her eyes they fell woefully short.

Philip told her that in the last twelve months he had realised that she had come to mean so much to him. He told her of his fear that she would leave Barker's and that they would drift apart.

"What I am saying, Mary, is that I am in love with you, so there it is. It feels such a relief and so good now that I have finally told you." He gazed down at the grass as he continued, "I have no intention of rushing into anything, but this weekend has just convinced me how comfortable we are in each other's company and, for the time being, it would be nice if we could do things like this more often, and just take it from there."

Mary was surprised by how calm and collected she was. She reached across and took his hand, entwining their fingers as she did. "You've said enough," was her reply as she gazed directly into his eyes, "I have always thought the world of you so ask me out anytime you like, and don't worry, the answer will always be yes." She gave him a big, wide smile which said more than a thousand words, before kissing him gently on the lips.

The train journey back to Chesterton was uneventful as they both quietly contemplated their weekend together, and wallowed in the warmth of their revealed feelings for each other. Philip had parked his car at Chesterton Station and before taking Mary back to Crest Hill, they called at his house for coffee. They shared again the memories of their weekend, something they would do again and again in the years to come, until it became almost surreal, almost as if something so wonderful must surely have been a dream.

Aunty Jo was still up as Mary let herself into the barn. She was bursting to tell her about all the exciting things she had seen, and the wonderful time she had had but Aunty Jo beat her to it.

"Well, how did your dirty weekend go?" was her opening shot.

"Aunty Jo, that's a horrible thing to say so I will treat it with the contempt it deserves. It's your dirty mind you want to bother about, not my fabulous weekend which I've enjoyed so much and you've just tried to spoil."

"Alright, alright," said Aunty Jo, "I'm sorry, but what's going on, our Mary, how do you stand with this Philip Manders?"

"Well, I'll tell you," replied Mary. "If, as a way of putting it, you ask me if we are going out, the answer is yes, because I am going to the Harvest Supper with him at the end of next month, if that's alright with you. If you ask me if I love him, the answer is yes – very, very probably I do. Now that's all I'm telling you so ask no more questions and you'll hear no lies, OK?" Then she went to bed.

As the next few weeks passed by, Mary and Philip drew closer together, their lives revolving more and more around each other. Barely a day went by when they did not meet, with either Mary popping into the office for a cup of tea, or Philip calling at the farm to check up on everyone's welfare, and on the days they didn't meet, they telephoned each other in the evening. Saturdays would see them dining in the Buttery Bar at the Golden Star Hotel in Chesterton where Mary had developed a taste for grilled Dover sole. Sunday was a day to walk across the fells, simply admiring the beauty of their surroundings, revelling in each other's company and in the deep, mutual affection they now shared.

Everyone who knew them, however remotely, had by now latched on to what was happening, and their association was met with almost total approval. 'What a smashing couple' and 'A match made in heaven' were some of the many comments.

There was the odd shaft of cynicism. "That Philip Manders has got his eye to business hooking up to her, all that land and cash in the background, he's no fool is he?" These were the remarks of a not particularly successful or popular farmer in the Market Bar one Tuesday. The general consensus, however, was that Philip and Mary were good for each other and, given Mary's age, it was about time she came down off the shelf!

"A woman as pretty as her, and with what her's achieved in her short life, 'ent going' to stay single fer ever, that's fer sure," was the reply from another farmer that met with nods of approval around the bar.

Aunty Jo, secretly quite pleased with how things were developing, said nothing but in her quieter moments she was glad that Mary was with someone she loved, and regularly prayed for her future happiness. She planned to wait for the right moment to vocalise her approval of the relationship, thus giving it her blessing. That moment was to come sooner than she thought!

Philip had taken great pains to befriend Billy, and whenever he visited the farm he always sought him out, greeting him with a cheery "How you doing, Bill?" whilst cuffing him playfully on the chin and ruffling his hair as he said it. He would shadow box round him, saying, "How do you fancy a few rounds with the Regimental Light Heavyweight Champion then, teach you a thing or two I would, young Bill?"

"Take no notice, Billy, he's telling lies – only thing he's ever been champion at is beer drinking," was Mary's contribution. It soon became noticeable that as Philip's car came into the yard, Billy would appear with a pleased expression on his face, eager to receive his greeting, and willing to take part in, and enjoy, the gentle ribbing he was about to receive. Billy loved the attention and simply grinned his way through it all.

At this time, however, something happened that was to have a profound effect on Billy's life. In very mysterious circumstances he acquired a dog, a small, smooth-haired Jack Russell Terrier. The little animal had two brown ears and a brown tail, with everything else being pure white. He had a cheeky character and a charm that had everyone saying what a smashing dog he was. Most importantly, he never left Billy's side, following him everywhere throughout the day, and then sleeping at the bottom of his bed at night.

Billy had found the dog in the top fields whilst scything down beds of stinging nettles. It was on Dick's instructions that he had walked up there one morning after all the stock had been fed, taking with him a bottle of water, a pork pie, and a piece of cake for his lunch.

"I'll pick you up in the truck, Billy, at five o'clock," Dick had told him and, as good as his word, he drove up the old track past Crest Pool and across the twenty acre field at five o'clock. He looked across the top field toward the spinney at the very peak of the hill and noticed, with some approval, the tidy headlands where Billy had worked the day long, scything down all the nettles, thistles, and docks that had been growing there. He then spotted Billy, his scythe on his shoulder, walking towards him with a little white dog following close to his heel.

"What have you got there, Billy," he asked. "Where's he come from?"

"I'se called him Binky," replied Billy, " an' he's bin 'ere all day. I jus' turned round this morning an' 'e was ther' so 'e's 'ad a bit of me pork pie an' a little drink out o' the ditch. 'E's mine now an' I'm tekkin' him hum wi' me."

"We'll see about that," said Dick, "somebody must have lost a nice little dog like that and he's going to be missed somewhere, I'll wager. Anyway, jump in and we'll see what our Mary and yer mom have to say about it."

Mary was aghast. "Somebody has either lost him or abandoned him, although I can't imagine anyone would abandon a dog like that."

Molly agreed. "He's a lovely little feller, I bet he can catch a rat an' all!"

"We must advertise in the *Ampleford Journal* next week in case anybody has lost him, and if nobody comes for him, you can keep him, Billy," Mary concluded.

"Whatever 'appens, 'e ent goin' nowhere, 'e's mine and I'm keepin' 'im, whatever 'appens, so ther!"

Mary could sense that Billy was already attached to the dog and silently prayed that no-one would answer the advertisement that was duly placed in the local paper. Happily no-one did so Binky and Billy went unseparated.

Billy's whole demeanour changed – for the first time in his life he had something that looked up to him, a living creature that obeyed his commands. He wasn't lonely anymore, and astounded everyone by identifying tasks that needed doing, and did them without instruction. Probably, more importantly, he now had something on which to lavish his affection, apart from his mother and Mary. His confidence soared, he had a newfound zest for life, and Mary was quietly loving to see it. 'Why,' she wondered, 'did we never think of getting him a dog before?'

Two weeks later, Mary and Billy, with Binky on his lap, were driving down to Chesterton to fetch some farming requisites – worming fluid and delousing powder – from the agricultural merchants there. They passed a gypsy family camped on the roadside grass verge with their Romany caravans, painted ponies, lurcher dogs, and grey washing laid across the hedgerow to dry.

"Gypsies, Billy, look a gypsy family, did you see them?"

"Ther' wuz one of 'em up the fields the other wik, an old lady all in black her wuz," Billy replied.

Mary caught her breath and her brain went into overdrive at Billy's reply. "Was that the day you were scything nettles and Binky came?" Mary enquired.

"Yer, I think it wuz, 'er wuz only ther' for a second an' 'er jus' vanished into the spinney."

For the first time in her life Mary almost lost her temper with him. "Billy, I could swing for you, I really could. We asked you umpteen times if you had seen anyone that day, or heard a car stopping in the track or anything and you said 'no, nothing'. Now you say you saw an old gypsy lady dressed in black."

"But 'er wuz only ther' fer a second, a long way off, and I wuzn't sure and I forgot anyway."

With Billy normally having a memory span of no more than an hour or two, Mary believed that he could have forgotten so she calmed down and decided to leave it at that. Nevertheless, for many years into the future, she often pondered and wondered if old Granny Harris had somehow contrived to give Billy the dog. She often looked at Binky thinking, 'Oh, how I wish you could talk, I reckon you would have one hell of a story to tell, little dog, but wherever you came from, I am so pleased that you are here.'

The following month Mary and Philip did go to the Harvest Supper, and a week later they went to St Mark's to the Harvest Festival Service. The church was decked, brimming with baskets of fruit, sacks of potatoes, big vegetable marrows, sheaves of corn, and a wonderful bread knot from the local bakery.

On the way down to church, Philip said to Mary, "I've got some news for you. We have received instructions from Elizabeth's mother to sell Crest Farm – the house, buildings, and four hundred acres. That will make you put your thinking cap on, I'll bet."

"Well, I've got some news for you," Mary replied. "I'm going to have a baby so you had better put your thinking cap on as well."

Philip gaped, and then his face broke into a broad smile. That smile was still on his face as, hand in hand, they walked through the church doors and made their way to the empty seats in the rear pews.

"I can't wait to tell the girls," he whispered.

During the service they sang the old harvest hymn:
Come ye thankful people come,
Raise the song of harvest home.
All is safely gathered in,
'Ere the winter storms begin.

'Yes,' thought Mary as she sat down, 'all is safely gathered in. Nearly all, but not quite all, not yet, anyway!'